LARGE
PRINT
EDITION

RANDOM
HOUSE

The New York Times
LARGE PRINT
Crossword Puzzle Omnibus

VOLUME

A COLLECTION OF 100 DAILY PUZZLES
EDITED BY
EUGENE T. MALESKA

Published by Random House Large Print

New York

Dedicated to
the memory of
Eugene T. Maleska

The New York Times

LARGE PRINT

Crossword Puzzle Omnibus

VOLUME

1

**SOLUTIONS TO THE PUZZLES
ARE FOUND AT THE BACK OF THE BOOK**

1

ACROSS

1 Like a good excuse
6 Christmas in Calais
10 Khayyám
14 Games
16 Public squares in ancient Rome
17 Biblical father and son
19 Golfer's concern
20 Colosseum section
21 Fool
22 Certain facts
23 ____ Na Na, singing group
24 Author Joyce Carol
27 Grand palace in Granada
32 Antonymous rhyme for fire
33 One North-South war
35 "____ armes!" (fighting words in France)
36 Biblical father and sons
39 Lawyer's thing
40 Francis or Dahl
41 Ancient Iranian
42 Smokers' needs
44 Nat and Natalie
45 Blue-chip initials
46 Ladd of film fame
48 Love, in Lucca
51 ____ Wojtyla (now Pope John Paul II)
53 Clay today
56 Biblical father and son
59 Word with air or house
60 Illusion created by magicians
61 Puppeteer Tony
62 Aqueduct action
63 Some in Rome are Spanish

DOWN

1 It flows into Africa's Orange
2 Prefix with dexterity
3 Angler's need
4 ". . . rose ____ rose": Stein
5 Zionist leader Jacob: 1872–1937
6 Argolic valley of games
7 Judah's wicked son
8 Catania's volcano
9 Hallucinogenic initials
10 "Anna and the King ____"
11 Sound of distress
12 Islands off Ireland
13 Sprightly or risqué
15 Trade center
18 Under control
22 Judge
23 Western classic starring 46 Across
24 Name at Tara
25 Assistants
26 Garbage
27 English composer and family
28 Built like a greyhound
29 Biblical tower
30 ____ la Paix
31 Car parts
33 Measure of gold's fineness
34 Unctuous
37 Transported in a dray
38 Egyptian deity
43 Like laborious work
44 Soprano Maria
46 Part of a foot of verse
47 Plunder
48 Fusses
49 Chart for Magellan
50 Completed
51 Patella site
52 It can be classified: Abbr.
53 Female friend in Fontainebleau
54 Chicago has a big one
55 ____ of Court
57 Priestly vestment
58 A Giant at 16

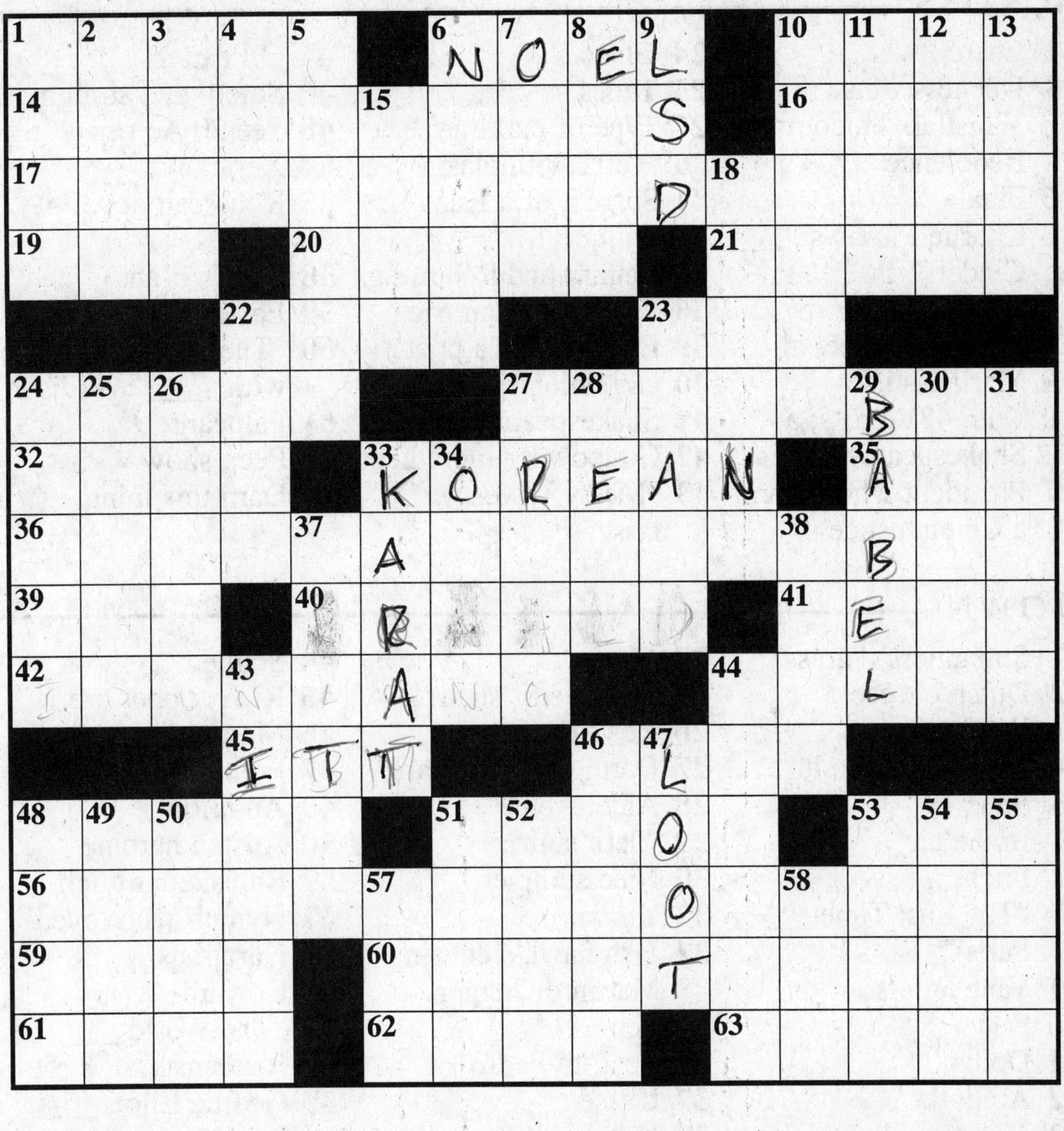

2

ACROSS

1 Lucre
5 Duchesse, e.g.
10 Whistlers on courts
14 Redolence
15 Finale
16 Charlie Plumb's "____ Cinders"
17 Asian staple
18 Mrs. Chaplin et al.
19 Marianas isle
20 With 48 Across, a Shakespearean line
23 President who became a Chief Justice
24 Glance
25 Tunes
27 Type of parking
30 Prefix with plasm
31 Subject of a Kant critique
33 Batman and Robin, e.g.
36 Shakespearean trio
39 Eternally, to a poet
40 Ukrainian river
41 Shakespearean villain
42 Gunpowder ingredient
43 "Merry Wives . . ." lass
44 Oil cartel
46 Safety and straight
48 See 20 Across
54 Xeric
55 Rousseau novel
56 Deesis
58 Bear's order
59 Eastern V.I.P.
60 "There is no living with ____": Addison
61 Fainéant
62 Peep show
63 Darn this thing

DOWN

1 Smugglers' "grass"
2 Dutch cheese
3 Wisdom
4 Area near the pit
5 Sneer
6 In the air
7 Pitch
8 "The Last Time ____ Paris"
9 Vane letters
10 Rue
11 Dodge
12 Ampulla
13 Houston
21 Western alliance initials
22 Gapes
25 Relative of smart
26 Road for Cato
27 Darth of "Star Wars"
28 Aide: Abbr.
29 Clark's girl
30 Nice summer
31 Uproar
32 Fish hawk's cousin
33 Martin or Jagger
34 Yen
35 Bear, to Pedro
37 Ukase
38 Metalworker
42 Pester
43 Pismire
44 Sculled
45 Rich copper ore
46 Martinique menace
47 French department
49 Audition
50 Austen heroine
51 Rathskeller quaff
52 Nymph who loved Narcissus
53 Coward
54 "The World ____ See It": Einstein
57 George Eliot, ____ Evans

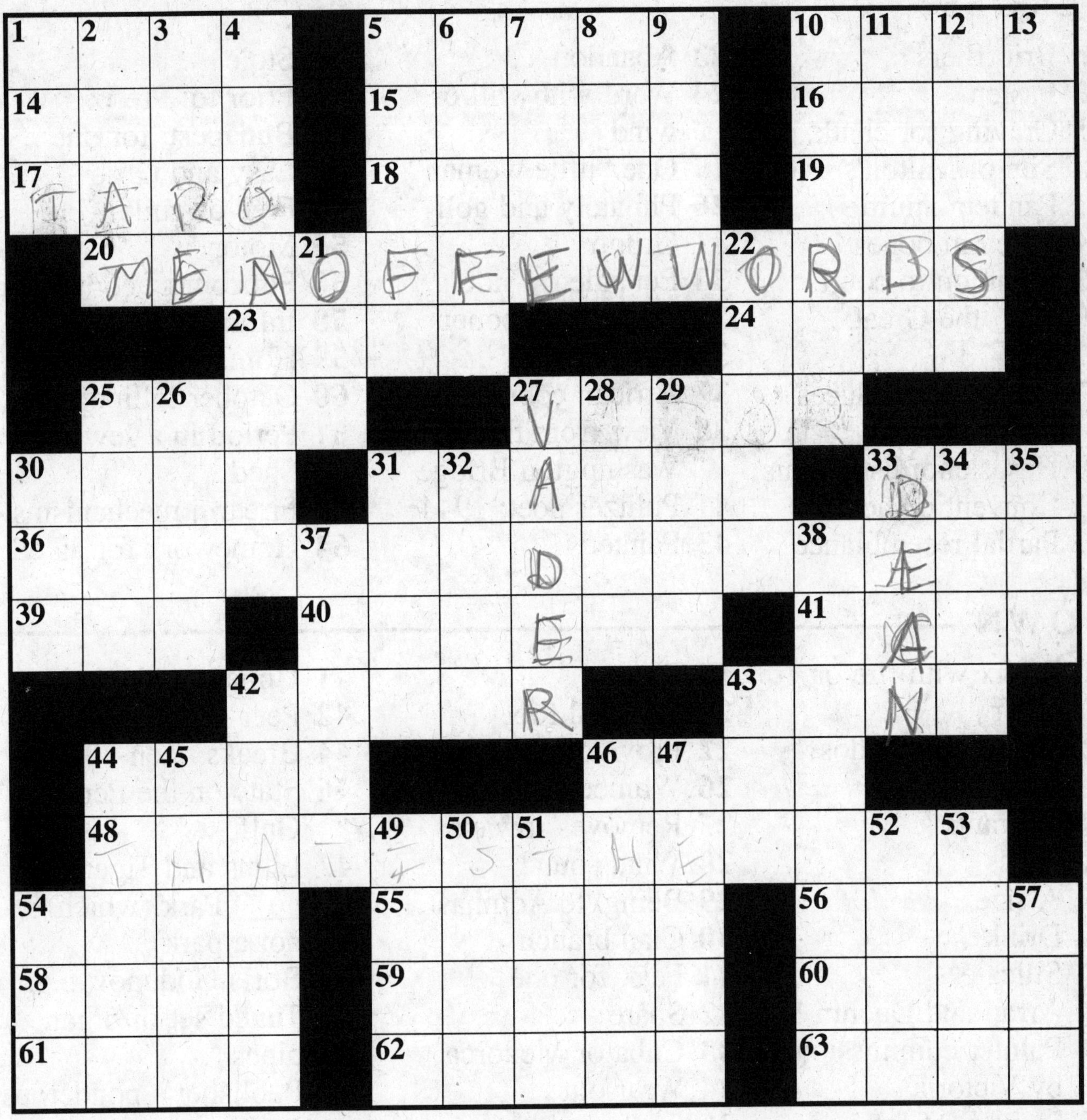
1 2 3 4 5 6 7 8 9 10 11 12 13
14 15 16
17 18 19
20 21 22
23 24
25 26 27 28 29
30 31 32 33 34 35
36 37 38
39 40 41
42 43
44 45 46 47
48 49 50 51 52 53
54 55 56 57
58 59 60
61 62 63
TARO
MENOFFEWWORDS
VADER
DEAN

3

ACROSS

1 Brit. fliers
4 Fasten
9 Craving for chalk, e.g.
13 Site of Milton's Pandemonium
14 Forearm bones
15 Summon to court
16 ____ the Great: 912–73
17 Palm that produces nuts
18 Harpsichordist Kipnis
19 Convention activity
21 Partial resemblance
23 Abandon
24 Word with will or wind
25 One "little woman"
26 Philately and golf
31 Grimp
34 Put side by side
35 D.D.E.'s opponent
36 Pickets
37 African cobra
38 View from the George Washington Bridge
41 Pulitzer poet: 1944
43 Painted
44 Stole
45 Prior to: Prefix
46 Budapest, for one
50 Easy and Grub
54 Free of guile
55 Motor
56 Puts out of competition
58 Information
59 Home of the Hawks
60 October lollipop
61 Period in a Jewish year
62 Shed
63 Firearm mechanisms
64 Homework for an ed.

DOWN

1 Prefix with fire or choir
2 Where a sacerdos presides
3 Vagrants
4 Cross
5 A size
6 Drink
7 Silicate
8 Arrau and Duchin
9 Painter commissioned by Victoria
10 Symbol of false friendship
11 Stop up
12 Ethereal
13 Dance
20 Metrical foot
22 Province in Can.
26 Whined
27 Removes rowans
28 Wind sound
29 Being, to Aquinas
30 Clan branch
31 Fear, for one
32 Spare
33 Cuba or Menorca
34 Wear out
36 Loose outer garments
39 Tie Pauline on a track
40 Withered, to George Wither
41 Umiak or shell
42 Peer's realm
44 Breaks open
46 State on the Persian Gulf
47 Lions and Tigers
48 ____ Park (which is not a park)
49 Boris Godunov, e.g.
50 Tuned set of organ pipes
51 Publisher's ponderous product
52 Old Norse poem
53 Trustworthy
57 Place for gobs of gobs

4

ACROSS

1 Quarrels
7 Pertain
13 Dixie river
15 Former Soviet republic
16 Changed into gaseous form
17 Horseshoe throws
18 "Cap'n ____," Lincoln novel
19 Polliwog
21 ____ Tyler, English rebel
22 Rivals of the Dodgers
24 Tourist attraction in Pompeii
25 Wait
26 Condition
28 One of three in "cyclic"
29 Musician of '76
30 Sign of coryza
32 Type of scholar
34 Exist
35 Experienced
36 Thatcher et al.
39 Pusher's customer
42 Tommy Dorsey favorite
43 Lew Wallace hero
45 Show disdain
47 Where Sligo is
48 Dark brown
50 Thrive
51 ____ Jacinto
52 Periods
54 Pious person, in Paris: Abbr.
55 Paul Pry
57 Ocean swell
59 Dürer and Whistler, e.g.
60 Altar-bound
61 Places to stay
62 Winebibbers

DOWN

1 Frugal ones
2 Dry red beverages
3 Virginia river
4 Finnish port
5 Parcel's partner
6 Slander
7 Blows one's top
8 Water bird
9 Triangle side
10 Fish of the herring family
11 Scolding speeches
12 ____ Island in the Pacific
14 Cite as proof
15 Copenhagen coins
20 Slapstick staple
23 Soap ingredient
25 Auction action
27 Strange
29 Certain pens
31 Zuider ____
33 Trough
36 Italian gulf
37 S.A. river
38 Tailor's tool
39 Melodic
40 Bouquet for a belle
41 Meadowlands performer
42 ____ Marco Polo
44 High points
46 Fall apparel
48 Foresighted fellows
49 Concerning
52 Small barracuda
53 Pudding starch
56 Exclamations
58 Interstice

5

ACROSS

1 ". . . with the greatest of ____"
5 Newscaster Lindstrom
8 Resounded
12 Novel by Durrell
13 Ankara citizens
15 Birthstone for 19 Across
16 G.B.S. play
19 Indian summer mo.
20 Sharp rebukes
21 Beat at Belmont
22 Chorine
23 Analyze sentences
24 "Upon my soul!" is one
26 Antediluvian
27 "For ____ a jolly good fellow . . ."
30 Highlander's shoulder covering
31 Guinea or Rock Cornish
33 Emitted, with "forth"
34 Shoemakers' gear
35 Finis
36 Ladder rung
37 Construction workers, of a sort
38 Ripen
39 Kind of card
40 Mystery writer Josephine
41 Berliner's article
43 Snow in Miami
45 Visit often
47 Tinted
48 Complied with
50 Stiff bristle
51 Lillie or Arthur
54 Joseph Conrad story
57 Weed in a grain field
58 Fatigued
59 Word of regret
60 Wee leftovers
61 Where mdse. is sold
62 Oversupply

DOWN

1 She doted on Narcissus
2 Guinness
3 Pew, for one
4 Spike of corn
5 Medal
6 Angers
7 Alias
8 Haley opus
9 ". . . clean hands, and ____": Psalm 24
10 Space Age acronym
11 Narrow valley
13 Transports for skiers
14 Scandinavian toast
17 Three-toned chords
18 Aptly named painter of ranch scenes
22 Charleston breakfast dish
23 Welty novel, with "The"
24 Carpenter's tool
25 John Patrick play, with "The"
28 Agent on a mission
29 Bit of marginalia
30 City map
32 U.K. division
33 Solemn
36 Lightning bolt
41 Work for piano and violin
42 Provide with income
44 "The Singing Cowboy"
46 Film actor Lew
48 "____ be in England . . .": Browning
49 Tolerate
50 Neighbor of Wyo.
51 Nautical time signal
52 Rebekah's hirsute son
53 Kind of prof.
55 Not masc. or neut.
56 Racing has-been

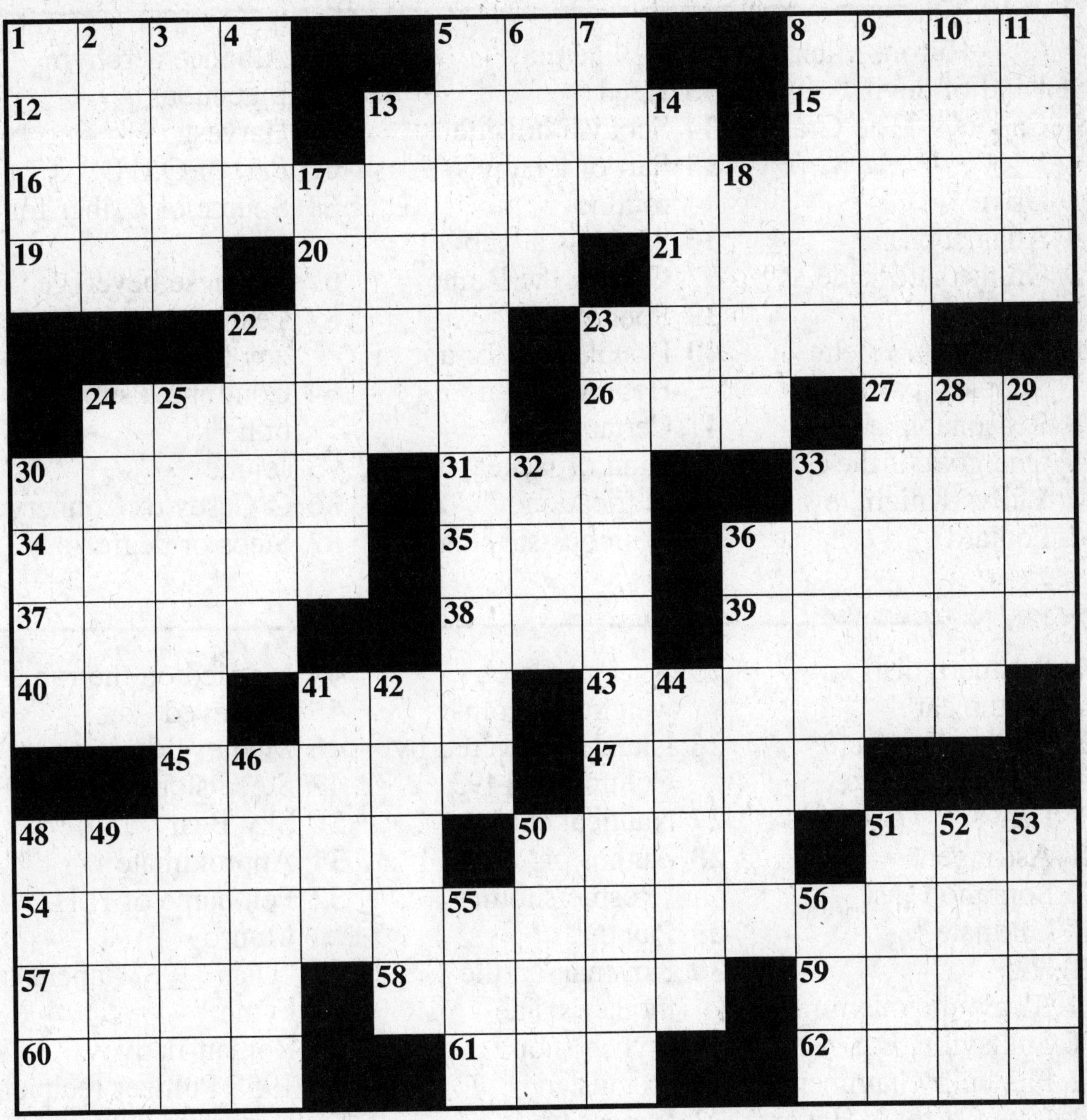

6

ACROSS

1 ____ Huron, Mich.
5 Kind of devil
9 Capote's "The Grass ____"
13 Drive
14 Atlas abbr.
15 On the safer side at sea
16 Bryant or Gillette
17 Simple's partner
18 Reasonable
19 One goal of the E.P.A.
22 Willys-Knight, e.g.
23 Foulard
24 Belligerence
33 Heed
34 Scottish hillside
35 Part of a baby's routine
36 Spun, as a web
37 City on the Rhine
39 Sound
40 Double this for a Hebrew hymn
41 Certain
42 Kind of jacket
43 Extrication
48 Resinous substance
49 Alliance acronym
50 Ingenuous
59 Harvest
60 Part of Q.E.D.
61 Source of a fiber for rope
62 Japanese beverage
63 Lear's consuming emotion
64 Continue a subscription
65 Jejune
66 O'Casey or Connery
67 Steps or degrees

DOWN

1 Southern dish
2 Of the ear
3 Newspaper sect.
4 Medium's state
5 Leave
6 Astringent
7 Soprano Grist
8 Ultimate
9 Hie
10 Kirgiz mountain range
11 Splitsville, U.S.A.
12 Flatten by hammering
13 Like Carroll's Hatter
20 "Tall, ____ and terrific"
21 Comfort, in Cannes
24 Intimidated
25 Ancient Greek weights or coins
26 Island discovered by Columbus: 1493
27 Nautical chain
28 Author of "Rosmersholm"
29 Pay dirt
30 Kinsman on the mother's side
31 Stylish shop
32 Exhausted
37 Messes up
38 Heavenly Altar
39 Haw's partner
41 Retort irritably
44 Married on the run
45 Achieved
46 Medieval lyric poem
47 Steep slope
50 Sky Bear
51 Approximate
52 Pen name of H.H. Munro
53 "Dies ____," ancient hymn
54 Roman-fleuve
55 1958 Pulitzer recipient
56 Distinctive flavor
57 Twilights
58 Morning moisture

7

ACROSS

1 Prefix with tasse
5 Aphid, e.g.
9 Former Turkish military title
14 Molecular part
15 Frequent follower of for
16 Tremulous
17 "Ship of the desert"
19 Soothing word
20 Amorous song
21 Pigment containing iron oxide
22 Senator from Kansas
23 Poet who wrote "The Faerie Queene"
24 Lightweight carriage
27 Give a wide berth to
28 Relative of a mesa
29 Players' stock
35 Let forth
36 Savanna
37 Top of a cliff
38 Lengthwise on a lighter
42 Please a gourmand
43 Strong vapor
44 Where matches are brought to thousands
46 Kind of butterfly
50 Rarae ____
51 Spread through, causing gradual change
52 Game bird
56 He played alongside Mantle
57 Irregular soldier
58 Public notice
59 Site of a Vichy French naval defeat: 1940
60 Galley gear
61 Naps
62 Accommodations at hostels
63 Pens' business ends

DOWN

1 Pops
2 To be, in Boulogne
3 Secure, as with cables
4 Closest
5 Cyclist
6 Foil a would-be catcher
7 Parched
8 Experiment
9 Like Griselda
10 Pale
11 Sir Patrick of ballad fame
12 Industrial center in Germany
13 Approaching, in poesy
18 TV program
21 Stimulus
23 Bundle, as of papers
24 Musical symbol
25 ____ sapiens
26 Moslem commander
27 Hold forth
30 Follower of box or marsh
31 Monomaniac's problem
32 Site of Mount Demavend
33 Ecclesiastical court
34 Lambs' mothers
39 Retards
40 Glowing gas
41 Grogshops
45 Back seat
46 Gantry
47 Civil War general
48 Juliet's fiancé
49 Put out bag and baggage
50 Forward or onward
52 Word after simon
53 Jai ____
54 Body established in F.D.R.'s day
55 Former Soviet news agency
57 U.S.N. tar

8

ACROSS

1 Fine violin
6 "And every ____ a queen": Kingsley
10 Supplicate
14 Discharge a Tommy
15 Skewed
16 Trick
17 Old-womanish
18 Scotland, to a poet
20 Odds and ends
22 Whirlybird
23 Neither Rep. nor Dem.
24 Afflict
25 Caballeros' partners
28 Asia Minor, once
33 ____ Alto
34 Seed covering
35 Tear
36 Hodgepodge
37 Salad ingredient
38 Carnegie of influence
39 Antiaircraft missiles
40 Caen's river
41 Smooth
42 Ireland, to Livy
44 Showy heron
46 Balaam's rebuker
47 Tar's milieu
48 Obvious
52 Harangues
57 Julius Caesar's conquest of 56 B.C.
59 Permissible
60 "The ____ of the Screw": James
61 Average
62 Spenser's name for Ireland
63 Relative of a cod
64 The others
65 Plus

DOWN

1 Huxtable and Rehan
2 Carte
3 Cole Porter's "I ____ Love"
4 Related
5 Ancient Hispania
6 Spiked the punch
7 Last of a Stein line
8 Musical tone
9 Shopper stoppers
10 Telephone onstage
11 Dwarfish animal or plant
12 Orient, to Napoleon
13 Circle of the seasons
19 Dummkopf
21 Elected ones
24 Fragrant seed
25 Lama leader
26 Out on ____
27 Largest of the deer family
28 Sphere of struggle
29 Ham and cheese on rye, e.g.
30 Permission
31 Ria
32 Arabian trading port in Roman times
33 Like Buckingham Palace
34 Molding edge
37 M. Kennedy's "The ____ Nymph"
43 Yawp
44 Common Market: Abbr.
45 It was divided "in partes tres"
47 Sordid
48 Orbit
49 ____ fortis (nitric acid)
50 Young ____ (radical)
51 "____ kleine Nachtmusik": Mozart
52 Word with need or consequences
53 Publicizes
54 Frozen desserts
55 Part of U.M.W.
56 E.r.a. or r.b.i.
58 Classic Japanese drama

9

ACROSS

1 Chits
5 Do a parent's job
9 Limited amount of time
13 "A part to tear ____ in": Shak.
14 Manx's relative
15 Scintillated
16 Baptism, e.g.
17 Item in many still lifes
18 Part of a Dante opus
19 Cleaves
21 Opera star Alda
23 Some scares for Dick Weber
25 Signed a contract
26 Range of influence
28 Suspenseful
30 Word of consolation
31 Red and Black
32 Like one side of Luna
36 "Cabaret" lyricist
37 Grew crops in a fixed order
40 Merry, in Avignon
41 Autocrat
43 Hebrew letters
44 "Grandfather Stories" author
46 Not ____ in the world
48 Stock-market declines
49 Sunnite deity
51 Fix rattan furniture
53 Outstanding, as a performance
55 Hammett whodunit, with "The"
58 Lag behind
59 ____ Rios, Jamaica
61 1953 Pulitzer Prize playwright
62 Lower-echelon personnel
63 Spread
64 Author Ephron
65 Rockfish
66 Brimming
67 Punkie

DOWN

1 "G.W.T.W." setting
2 Kind of rain
3 Mother of Solomon
4 More sharply sloped
5 Legendary equestrian
6 Cover one's traces
7 Beast that balks
8 Coral ridge
9 Hit the golf ball with the heel of the club
10 City in Puerto Rico
11 Paid for a hand
12 Modernists
15 What a radar beam does
20 Thinner in density, as gases
22 Hair treatment
24 Shore-dinner tidbit
26 Directive to a typesetter
27 Degs. for would-be Kants
29 Highway sign
31 Ending for hip or poll
33 Father of Electra
34 Storm
35 Oversized chocolate chip
38 Mid-American Indian
39 Lama of renown
42 Auto races
45 Collection agency's tactic
47 Directions to square dancers
48 Dolphin colony
49 Roman villa features
50 Clues
52 A Kennedy
53 Puncture
54 Mouth part
56 Taj Mahal site
57 Undiluted, as whisky
60 Actor Gulager

10

ACROSS

1 Where St. Paul was shipwrecked
6 Tabula ____
10 Not of the clergy
14 Kind of artery or vein
15 Ancient kingdom on the Persian Gulf
16 Part of an estate
17 Small, silvery food fish
18 Enchanted
20 Political party meetings
22 Photographer's word
23 Leaping light
24 What F.D.R. said he hated
25 Kind of dome in a Texas team's home
28 Ricochets
33 Pewter, for one
34 "Praise ye the Lord!"
35 Enter
36 Gambling game using 40 cards
38 Word with sum
39 Like a siren
41 "Ars gratia ____"
42 Expedient
43 Kind of furnace
44 Hwy.
45 Poetic pugilist
46 Quick as ____
50 ____ Mountains, near the Black Sea
55 Spot for a 9-year-old
57 "____ ear and out . . ."
58 Exude
59 Incumbent on
60 Val d'____, Italian Alps resort area
61 They caught Dillinger
62 Like Cassius
63 Snub

DOWN

1 File sect.
2 Sir Lawrence ____-Tadema, English painter
3 Stead
4 Household powder
5 Risk calculator
6 Old minstrel's instrument
7 Brews
8 Maxim
9 Friendly
10 Intertwine
11 Yearn
12 Angers
13 Homophone for seed
19 Spasm or pang
21 "No seats" sign
24 Strip of shoe leather
25 "All ____," early Berlin song
26 Incisions
27 Jealous suitor in "Pagliacci"
28 Place for a home
29 Beyond: Prefix
30 Berlioz's "Les ____ d'Eté"
31 "The butler ____"
32 Alleges
33 Sun, to skin
36 Merry
37 Formerly
40 Imprecation
41 De Larrocha and Markova
43 Italian navy
45 Copland
46 Atwitter
47 Kipling's "____ Sea to Sea"
48 Idle
49 Gulf of ____, Arabian Sea arm
50 ____ figure (attract attention)
51 Ever's partner
52 Not so hot
53 "Once more ____ the breach": King Henry V
54 Kind of belt
56 Unclose, to Coleridge

11

ACROSS

1 Now
6 Emulate James F. Fixx
9 Noggin
13 Get on a soapbox
14 Makes ____ day (delights)
16 Forever ____ day
17 Spanish kings
18 Pop song by the Beatles
20 Moslem religion
21 "____ child has to work . . ."
22 Olympic god
24 Kin of day rooms
25 Where a chemist may spend the day
27 Space agcy.
29 Braggart
34 Desire
36 Foremost painter of Spanish national customs
38 Pester
39 Bacteria that die without free oxygen
41 Ariel
43 Stone monument
44 Canzones
46 Dogboat
47 Avant-courier
49 Size
51 Govt. agency
52 ____ Day (Annunciation)
54 He loves, to Ovid
56 "____ Time," TV show
61 Suit to
64 "____ Ice," 1965–69 show
65 Lowest point
66 Part of the eye
67 Singer Turner
68 Hang loosely
69 City on the Irtysh
70 Turner of a best seller
71 Up to now

DOWN

1 Convex moldings
2 Paco and galena
3 Worker for wages
4 On ____ (carousing)
5 Sycophants
6 Pleasures
7 Pharmacy directive
8 P.C. Wren's "Beau ____"
9 "A ____ Day's Night," Beatles song
10 "En ____ Natt," Ingrid Bergman film: 1938
11 "Queen for ____"
12 Doris and Dennis
15 Bitten
19 Synthetic
23 Judicious
25 Restraint
26 Crest in the Dolomites
28 Nothing to write home about
30 Bishoprics
31 Retire
32 Sir William of Canada
33 Requires
35 Alone onstage, as Scotto
37 Ripener
40 "When Day Is Done" is one
42 On the Baltic
45 Beach city of racing fame
48 "A ____ the Races," Marx Brothers film
50 Blake of "Gunsmoke"
53 Have one's ____ court
55 Hebrew months
56 Where Dayton is
57 Comic Crosby
58 Their mascot is a bulldog
59 Thin, flat, circular object
60 Med. school subject
62 Put in a waterline
63 Waste allowance

12

ACROSS

1 Adjective once misapplied to the Earth
5 Like Ferdinand or Isabella
10 One of Niña's gaffs
14 Coin for a descendant of Columbus
15 Obliterate
16 Mata ____
17 Italian navigator: 1454–1512
20 One concern of a skipper
21 Maria and Clara
22 Garden tool
23 "____ we forget"
24 Columbus was one
28 Confined
29 ____ Amin, Grand Mufti of Jerusalem
32 Caper
33 A Pinta officer
34 Like Lindbergh's flight
35 Where Columbus died: 1506
38 And others: Latin abbr.
39 College or collar
40 Enveloping glows
41 ____ Plaines, Ill.
42 Jeanne and Cécile: Abbr.
43 Australian lumbermen
44 Where Vientiane is
45 Actor Linden
46 Columbus's first ____ to Spain was made on the Niña
49 Columbus, by birth
54 Parader in October
56 Blue dye
57 Language of millions in India
58 Narrated
59 Bando, Maglie and Mineo
60 Prominent Alaskan family
61 Antarctica is devoid of these

DOWN

1 British tart
2 This gives ade
3 San Salvador's 60 square miles
4 Boat covering, for short
5 Tract
6 What seas do to shores
7 Donated
8 Enzyme
9 Decreased
10 Sidetrack
11 NATO is one
12 Old chest for valuables
13 "The Making of an American" is his autobiography
18 Whence Odysseus sailed
19 What 1492 is part of
23 Admit
24 Rescued
25 Growing out
26 Cartographer's volume
27 Place on the Floss
28 Whence Columbus sailed
29 Viscount Templewood
30 "____ needs a good memory": Quintilian
31 Founder of U.S. Navy tradition
33 Specks
34 Revolved rapidly
36 Explode
37 Martín Alonso Pinzón, e.g.
42 Rani's gown
43 Discussion groups
44 Periods of calm
45 Surround
46 Inlets; creeks
47 Sicilian menace
48 Kind of wind
49 Navigator Vasco da ____
50 Life, to Columbus
51 A social sci.
52 Ancient mariner
53 Bow and stern, e.g.
55 Gee-gee

13

ACROSS

1 Covenant
5 Mail rte.
8 Counterpart
13 "Woe is me!"
14 Greek underground org. of W.W. II
16 Gem State
17 Gold-rush center in 1900
18 Clod
19 Eminent
20 Economists' stat.
21 S.A. plant growing in mountainous regions
23 Mar
25 Pharaohs
26 Hercules' captive
27 Mount
28 Pomme de ____
30 Young fellows
31 Pewter ingredient
34 Turkish imperial standard
35 Age or wall leader
37 Glazier's need
38 "My country, ____ . . ."
39 Bold Bidder, to Spectacular Bid
40 Bedouin
41 Nobelist Pauling
42 Kind of hole or show
43 Gadget
45 Pontificates on a platform
47 Colonial civil servant
49 Bosh!
51 Day's march
52 Vittles
53 Cartagena child
54 Upper air
55 Galley mark
56 Site of Vance A.F.B.
57 Hampton ____
58 B'way sign
59 Old oath

DOWN

1 Throe
2 Isolated
3 Gathering places for certain scouts
4 Monogram of Prufrock's creator
5 Fasten anew, as boots
6 Water chute
7 Moist
8 Intermixes
9 Emulated Héloïse
10 Language spoken around Kazan
11 The mating game
12 Scuttles
15 Athenian's rival
21 Wan
22 Napped leather
24 Race-track bettor's consideration
27 Blackthorns
28 Make trimmings
29 Biblical prophet
31 Meddler's activity
32 ____ tizzy
33 Sparks of old flicks
35 Moses' mountain
36 Plods
37 Frost or Burns
39 Furtive movers
40 Stingy
41 Truncated
42 Quickly
43 Moro chief
44 Triple Crown winner: 1935
45 Mink's kin
46 "Crime and Punishment" character
47 Groucho expression
48 Cloches or toques
50 Mary ____ Lincoln
53 Born

14

ACROSS

1 Pop
5 Bundles
10 Contest at Belmont
14 Enthusiasm
15 Gothic arch
16 Mine entrance
17 Whitewall, e.g.
18 Consumer advocate
19 Tease
20 A beginning
23 Portion
24 Where Caesar trod
25 Offshoot
28 Like Harvard's "Pudding"
31 Gasp
32 Winding
34 Skip over water
37 Slightly more than never
40 "____ and Sympathy"
41 Chatter, with "on"
42 Kind of eye
43 Storms
44 Rank
45 Regimen
47 "Rubáiyát" poet
49 Finally
55 Manitoban Indian
56 Two on the aisle
57 Toy-bear hero
59 Former Celtics star
60 Fences in
61 Pulitzer Prize playwright: 1953
62 Glut
63 Nettlesome
64 Broadway gas

DOWN

1 Coterie
2 Hodgepodge
3 Mild oath
4 Short narrative
5 Plus
6 Yawning
7 Playground of Venice
8 Kind of number
9 Curative agents
10 Curio
11 ____ a dozen
12 Autumn beverage
13 Season in Chartres
21 Eternity
22 Boxer's pinnacle
25 Detect
26 Support of a sort
27 Quechuan Indian
28 Sword handles
29 Botanical exterior
30 Umpire's call
32 Bottleneck
33 Potter's paste
34 Teresa Stratas, e.g.
35 In the thick of
36 Soccer great
38 Seething with indignation
39 Diamondback
43 What some hairlines do
44 Slender fish
45 Andrea ____
46 Passive
47 Repeatedly
48 Cryptogamous
50 Nile killers
51 Lowest high tide
52 Surrealist painter
53 Kind of eagle or wolf
54 Trademark
55 TV initials
58 Party member of a sort

15

ACROSS

1. Thick piece
5. Reading, e.g.
9. Diminish
14. Chanel
15. Bullets, etc., for short
16. Panamanian city
17. Publisher Adolph
18. City on the Truckee
19. Hollywood employee
20. Emlyn Williams play
23. Word with flower or water
24. Entry in a teacher's roll bk.
25. Young member of a pride
29. Dutch disease victim
31. Dir. from Zurich to Lucerne
34. Port in Caesar's day
35. Ratite bird
36. Companion of tear
37. Salinger opus
40. "Just ____ doch-an'-dorris": Lauder
41. Electrical unit
42. Choreographer Ailey
43. Small ape
44. Pompous one
45. Bits of land in water
46. Edict of a sort
48. Holder of an LL.B.
49. "Oats, peas, ____ grow," start of a nursery jingle
57. Yellowstone Park denizens
58. Musical ending
59. Bog
60. Grand
61. Imposing work
62. Rail
63. A Ford
64. Secretary, e.g.
65. Oriental maid

DOWN

1. Dundee native
2. Ness or Lomond
3. Word with head or tooth
4. Brown pear
5. Attic
6. Improve
7. Prefix with potent or present
8. She wrote "A Girl Like I"
9. Bitter
10. Emulates Larry Holmes
11. Der ____ (Adenauer)
12. Rent
13. Spanish queen before Sophia
21. West Indian sorcery
22. Range
25. Kind of train or government
26. "____ ship a-sailing . . ."
27. Aquatic mammal
28. Riviera resort
29. Jannings and Ludwig
30. Imparted
31. Tennis play
32. Berlin's "____ with Music": 1921
33. British naval women
35. Antithesis of Eris or Ares
36. In good health
38. Mary Ann ____ (George Eliot)
39. "____ la vista!"
45. "Give ____ to the Indians," 1939 song
46. Lighter
47. Photographer Adams
48. ____ Ababa
49. Gun sight
50. Pitcher parts
51. Made a hole-in-one
52. Slangy negative
53. Ponselle or Bonheur
54. Weaver's gear
55. Actor Stone
56. Opposite of 52 Down
57. Breton grain

16

ACROSS

1 Keystone ____
5 Sir, in Delhi
10 Monster
14 Fitzgerald
15 Word with glass or house
16 Stomach
17 Horsing around, in "Equus"?
19 Fogginess
20 Longest river in Scotland
21 Asian weight
22 Little Jack ____
24 Bettor's note
26 Rickenbacker, e.g.
28 Foundation
29 Swindles
31 Have games with Pogo's team?
35 Korbut
36 Like bone
37 Unite
38 European subways
40 Giants of myth
42 Opposite of hurrah
43 Rope fibers
47 Velvet and army followers
48 Unassisted putout?
50 Report-card time, to some
51 Chapel monk
52 Mountain
53 Snake
54 Aspen activity
57 Electric-company customer
59 Rented
62 On one's ____ (alert)
63 Where to look up "Hamlet"?
66 Kin of lui
67 Some looks
68 Wildcat
69 Protection for goalies
70 Out
71 River into the Elbe

DOWN

1 Held on to
2 Pot for puchero
3 Out in left
4 Declare
5 Oriental bean
6 Pleads
7 Vixen
8 Biblical captain
9 Former Senator Birch ____
10 Pigments for Opie
11 Catches in the upper deck?
12 Tear down
13 Jug
18 Heat unit, for short
23 Old European coins
25 Glacial ridges
27 CBS logo
29 Bass, sax and guitar
30 New York city
31 Presume
32 Victim of a scam
33 Wyoming county
34 In disorder
39 Italian tongue
41 Little fellows
44 Watering place in Belgium
45 Refers (to)
46 Some sinners
49 Gets up
53 Humorist Bill
54 Footprint
55 Caffeine nut
56 Swallow
58 Gaelic
60 Novel name
61 Rasputin's ruler
64 A.F.T. rival
65 Don Ho adornment

17

ACROSS

1 Ruth's native land
5 Stitched
9 Rhyme scheme
13 This place has a lock on New Haven
14 Number in a tub
15 Frond bearer
16 One of Blake's "Songs of Innocence"
19 Color
20 Lubricated
21 Ransack
22 ____ qua non
23 Part of a min.
24 Place "above the fruited plain"
31 Largest of seven
32 Prayer
33 Gist
35 Pair
36 Ring a bell
38 Means of self-defense
39 Posed
40 Mint
41 Argus galley
42 "Dilly dilly" followers in a song
47 Charles Schulz's need
48 Suffix with poet
49 Constructed
52 Wooden shoe
54 Buffalo's relative
57 Rarely
60 Sapphic songs
61 Glowing coal
62 First of the James Bond films
63 Palos, once
64 Garden vegetable
65 Twist

DOWN

1 Orpheus-Eurydice tale, e.g.
2 Honolulu's island
3 To the sheltered side
4 Spelldown
5 Author Asch
6 Canal, lake or city
7 One of the Slavs
8 Opposite of pos.
9 Second largest of seven
10 Bouillon base
11 Memorable Belgian musician
12 Maxwell Anderson heroine
14 "To ____ own self be true": Shak.
17 Wind
18 Actress Nissen
22 Fokker fighter in W.W. I
23 Large knife of yore
24 Hippies' homes
25 Customary
26 Lariat in Laredo
27 State one's view
28 Danube city
29 Habituate
30 Gentle push
34 Benefit
36 Kin of bop
37 Concealed
38 Norse chieftain
40 Hundred: Comb. form
43 Of least worth
44 Cut of meat
45 Search hurriedly
46 Golden ____
49 Betty ____ of old comics
50 Solve a mystery
51 Bakery specialist
52 Identical
53 Cleric in Caen
54 Eponym for a great city
55 First-rate
56 Be cognizant of
58 Pen point
59 Elizabeth Blackwell's colleagues: Abbr.

18

ACROSS

1 Suggestion
5 "Caveat emptor" notice
9 "It's ____ country"
14 Voyaging on the QE2
15 Sewing-machine inventor
16 Settle down for the night
17 Salamander
18 Discordant
19 See 6 Down
20 "I have a ____": King
22 Unique individual
24 Jacques' summers
25 Alabama site of a Freedom March
26 Says
28 Sluggish
30 Lennon was one
34 Kind of sister
37 Mortise fitting
39 Like some infections
40 Outline
42 Soprano Galli-Curci
44 Coral island
45 Estimator
47 Peridot, e.g.
48 Mexican food
50 King Arthur's father
52 Pleasure-dome site, in a Coleridge poem
54 "____ again!"
58 Play parts
61 Move
62 Farm-equipment name
63 Weeping one
65 Physicist's abbr.
67 Throat impediment
68 "Roots" author
69 Movie pioneer
70 Icelandic literary works
71 Gotlander
72 Misses the ball
73 Nothing, in Nancy

DOWN

1 Field workers
2 French river
3 Stairway post
4 Straw mat
5 "Eureka!"
6 With 19 Across, famed black abolitionist
7 "____ Hold Your Hand," 1963 song
8 Ukrainian river
9 MOMA offering
10 Offshore flapper
11 Complete defeat
12 Tasso's patron
13 Suffixes with ordinal numbers
21 Conchita's cape
23 Johnny ____
27 Title for Jesse Jackson
29 Conger
31 Kin of geom.
32 Behind schedule
33 Ancient region, now part of Iran
34 Minor dispute
35 Jorge of baseball
36 Type of spar
38 Subject of a Styron book
41 Source of a yellowish oil
43 "____ Lady," T. N. Page short story
46 Official who checks accounts
49 Printers' measures
51 Illegal smoke
53 "____ told by an idiot . . .": Macbeth
55 "Rigoletto" composer
56 Wear down
57 Former Secretary of the Treasury
58 Exclamations from Hans
59 Bird's gullet
60 Mah-jongg piece
64 Sandwich bread
66 Cries of pain

19

ACROSS

1 Inverness is one
5 Kind of strip
10 Struck, old style
14 Across the plate
15 Seed
16 River in a canine's name
17 Gardner's lawyer-detective
19 Caesar's etymological cousin
20 Subject of a book by Adelaide Bry: 1976
21 Anguineous creatures
22 Not so prolix
24 Sometime partners of stars
25 First name of the 18th U.S. President
26 Identity documents
29 Hammett private eye
32 With 40 Across, a patriot
33 Visorless cap
34 Punty
35 Cut of meat
36 Passages for gas, steam, etc.
37 Chevet
38 Form for Frank Lloyd Wright
39 Plods, as through mud
40 See 32 Across
41 Stretch
43 Gripping tool
44 Forage plant
45 Licorice or parsnip
46 Laud
48 One of Adam's boys
49 Hood's quaff
52 ____ Kong
53 Spillane's slugging shamus
56 Setting for a gem
57 Heed Revere's warning
58 Home of the Hawks
59 Items in Trevino's bag
60 Slender candle
61 Blessing

DOWN

1 Clerical mantle
2 Some are rarae
3 Flibberti-gibbety
4 Commit a blooper
5 Promising ones
6 Athletic fields
7 Put into disorder
8 Intl. labor group
9 Small French coins
10 Petty ruler
11 Christie's gumshoe
12 Of wrath: Lat.
13 HI before 1959
18 Pine for
23 Formerly, formerly
24 One of the astronauts
25 Male red deer
26 West Indian volcano
27 Coral island
28 Van Dine's suave sleuth
29 Twilled fabric
30 Medicine applicator
31 Beautiful areas
33 Salvation Army founder
36 Dining table doily
37 Finished a flight
39 NCO's
40 Love, in Lanai
42 Whinnies
43 Commotion
45 A.F.B. in Texas
46 Unit of illumination
47 Libertine
48 Between hop and jump
49 Bullets and bombs, for short
50 Light, gauzy fabric
51 Milesian's land
54 A Gershwin
55 Kind of scene

20

ACROSS

1 Pops in Boston and elsewhere
5 Jai ____
9 Darkness; gloom
13 Prefix with poise
14 Sparkle
15 On the deep
16 Free spender from the sticks
19 Utter
20 Piquant
21 Sam or Remus
22 Journey that is no junket
23 Metric unit of area
24 Like a thank-you letter
31 Secular
32 Affects, as a virus
33 Friend for Fernand
34 Nursemaid in Calcutta
35 Substitute
37 Cordon bleu
38 Sun. follower
39 Wander
40 First-rate
41 Clumsy
46 Hairy creature
47 A side of New York
48 Thrash
51 What many hail in a hailstorm
53 Botanist Gray
56 Mrs. Cripps of a G. & S. operetta
59 City 200 miles south of Moscow
60 Family in a Wolfe novel
61 Amerinds of the West
62 Kind; sort
63 "____ take arms . . .": Hamlet
64 Peer

DOWN

1 Five-time Presidential candidate
2 Greenish blue
3 Customhouse levy
4 Command to Rover
5 Largest of 50
6 Fuzz
7 Singer Gibb
8 Resident of: Suffix
9 Lodestone
10 Seagoing org.
11 Actual
12 "Citizen ____"
14 Cupidity
17 "Cantos" author Pound
18 Spiritual guides
22 Part of M.I.T.
23 How adepts function
24 Creek or inlet
25 Pleasingly mirthful
26 Mother-in-law of Ruth
27 Fort ____, N.J.
28 Calif.-Nev. boundary lake
29 Alter; correct
30 Abounding
31 Shish kebab item
35 Part of the epidermis
36 Brit. answer to the Luftwaffe
37 Light delivery vehicle
39 Drive back
42 Tell on a classmate
43 Abutting
44 Manners of walking
45 To live, to Livy
48 Stain
49 Well ventilated
50 Pace
51 Ski lift
52 Pittypat in "G.W.T.W."
53 Transactions
54 Canal built by de Lesseps
55 Church part
57 Psyche component
58 Toupee: Slang

21

ACROSS

1 ____ forth (lectured)
5 To one side
10 Ideologies
14 Lake on the U.S.-Canadian boundary
15 News medium of yore
16 Noted navigator
17 Puccini heroine
18 Epigrammatic
19 Losing racer
20 Babushkas
22 Spirelike
24 Fisheye lens, e.g.
26 Knot
29 Geisha's waistband
30 Roundup item
34 Havens for sightseers
36 What a litterbug does
38 Skyways alien
39 "Eureka!"
41 Ashanti language
42 Pfc.'s, for example
43 Sparrowlike birds
46 Evergreen oak
48 Eydie's man
49 Word now on cigarette packs
51 Mitigated
52 Natives of Erivan
55 Mentor
58 Book signatures
62 Iranian coin
63 Michelangelo piece
65 Eliot's "Adam ____"
66 Wickerwork material
67 Places for troughs
68 Pulitzer Prize novelist: 1958
69 Conveyance without wheels
70 "Romantic Comedy" author
71 Quartz variety

DOWN

1 Encloses, with "in"
2 Gold-medalist Heiden
3 What Pizarro called "City of Kings"
4 Mythical maiden of Eire
5 French play divisions
6 Magician's word
7 Breeze
8 Set limits
9 Dutch ____
10 "____ the Wind," Lawrence and Lee play
11 Rise
12 Aging filly
13 Doff
21 "Our Town" personae
23 Apposite
25 Dictionary abbr.
26 Blackens
27 Dietary directive to J. Sprat
28 Make amends
31 Patronage
32 Threefold
33 Hafez al-____, Syrian President
35 "____ Wore a Yellow Ribbon," John Ford film
37 Fearful respect
40 Like the Alcan Highway
44 Helped
45 ____ Andreas fault
47 Winter melons
50 Created a major disturbance
53 Broods
54 ____ in point
55 Swings of a pendulum
56 Switch TV channels
57 Barometer's forerunner
59 Brightest star in Lyra
60 River to the Baltic
61 Kind of pearl
64 Perón or LeGallienne

22

ACROSS

1 Exults
7 Barbara Eden's target in a TV series
10 Hot spot
14 Not more than
15 Forage plant
16 Hoodwink
17 Left port
19 To be, in Paree
20 Puts down turf
21 Palmer's forte
23 Myerson's crown in 1945
24 Kind of upmanship
25 "___ long way to . . ."
29 Sharp
30 Come near, with "on"
32 Some warehousemen
34 Kin of sobrinas
35 Sends out again
36 "Don't give up ___"
39 Dye
40 Serves a sentence
41 Belief
43 Affected
44 Quarrel
45 Above, to F. S. Key
46 Device for stimulating emission of radiation
48 Superiority
51 Guam harbor
55 Repeat
56 Guidance
58 Swizzle
59 Be at fault
60 Home-grown
61 Some ophidians
62 Part of E.S.T.
63 Kind of "ship" with a franchise

DOWN

1 It bites in the Atlantic Bight
2 H.R.E. emperor
3 Word with ships
4 Saturates
5 Recipe amt.
6 Kind of rate or rocket
7 Showy flowers
8 ___ Doctrine: 1947
9 ". . . wagon to ___": Emerson
10 Pindarics
11 Byline information
12 Carson's "Silent ___"
13 Indian home
18 Keeps in check
22 Hosts of warships
25 Neighbor of Syr.
26 ___ dansant (tea dance)
27 Pinta to Santa Maria
28 Ant cow
29 Held on to
31 Positions in Goren's game
33 Flour made from corn, beans, etc.
34 "___ also serve . . ."
36 Sultry
37 "___ Yankee Doodle . . ."
38 Favorite
40 Extreme conservative
41 ___ cropper (fails)
42 Strikes back
43 Maintain
47 Cathedral city of France
49 High crags
50 ___ Oreille (Idaho lake)
51 Nick and Nora's terrier
52 Donahue of TV
53 Cleave
54 Mimic
57 Scottish explorer

23

ACROSS

1 Rum-and-water drink
5 ____ law, used by the Franks
10 Rebuff
14 "Hold ____ horses!"
15 Historic town in Iraq
16 Bustle
17 Mickey and kin
18 Countenance
19 Actor Skinner
20 Greet, in a way
23 Small drinks
24 Pique
25 Lose
28 Water plant
30 Bleak
33 Utopian
34 Region
35 River in Yorkshire
36 See 56 Across
39 Indian butter
40 Toward the mouth
41 Decided for
42 Goddess of the dawn
43 House at O.S.U.
44 Springs
45 Eur. country
46 Slammer
47 Words after "Fragile"
54 Shaped like a stadium
55 Headdress at Canterbury
56 With 36 Across, like a pinup man
58 ____-Lenape, Delaware Indian
59 Criminal offense
60 Madame Bovary
61 Yellowish-brown wool
62 Certain tides
63 Famed couturier

DOWN

1 Training ground for Larry Holmes
2 Louis XV and XVI
3 Cry of pain
4 Superior, e.g.
5 Two-point score in football
6 Baby sitters in Peking
7 Output of St. Helens
8 "____ City" (Pittsburgh)
9 General for whom a sweater was named
10 Author of "Oldtown Folks": 1869
11 Pen name used by Viaud
12 Mine passage
13 Like Buckingham Palace
21 Eucalyptus eater
22 Spanish Mme.
25 Tiny pest
26 Baking potato
27 Dry periods
28 Enlightened Buddhist
29 Conduct
30 Public disorders
31 Napoleon's "Grande" group
32 Devil's-trumpets, e.g.
34 Seaport in Spain
35 Drew in by suction
37 Eric the Red was one
38 Architectural order
43 Suffix with care
44 Site of the University of Georgia
45 Talk-show quip
46 Leather band
47 Where cargo goes
48 Assert
49 Darling dog
50 Fencing
51 "____ boy!"
52 Nerve branches
53 Patron saint of sailors
57 Gibbon

24

ACROSS

1 Greek letters
5 This precedes Baker
9 Does road work of a sort
14 "Ma, He's Making Eyes ____"
15 Fire's foe
16 Corvette's prey
17 Teen-ager's infatuation
19 "____ say die"
20 Mysterious obj. in the skies
21 Decorated the walls
23 French pronoun
24 Validate
26 Ache
28 Gear features
31 Leading man, now and then
34 Rueful exclamation
36 French cookbook word
38 Shadow: Comb. form
39 Matinee ____
40 Actress Saint's middle name
41 Sound from Tabby's "motor"
42 Third son of Jacob
43 Church part
44 Pinches
45 Massages
47 Crime causing a conflagration
49 Kind of preview
51 Claros or conchas
55 "Ulalume" author
57 Theater districts
60 Welcome ____
61 This may end a dream
63 Court score
65 Central Asian mountain system
66 Any letter in NATO
67 Clothes or family follower
68 Scratches out
69 Relatives of sens.
70 Tear

DOWN

1 Another name for New Guinea
2 Fill
3 ". . . ____ blind desire": Kipling
4 Follower of Aug.
5 Greatly excited
6 Betty of cartoons
7 Flow along or against
8 Kind of board
9 Fountain fare
10 Ribicoff
11 Trophy
12 Asian weight unit
13 Mus. group
18 Battle site in 1914, 1915 and 1917
22 Strange
25 Native of Leghorn
27 Grating upon
29 Kind of door
30 Brother of Hengist
32 What snobs put on
33 Conjunction
34 Arabian gulf
35 Parlor pieces
37 Rank
39 Sort
40 Kenyan native
44 Like blue jays and catbirds
46 Skin layer
48 Dred and Walter
50 Grain sorghum
52 Love, to 25 Down
53 Despoil
54 Bucephalus, for one
55 Former talk-show host
56 Highly seasoned meat dish
58 "The ____ Eagle"
59 Hockey foul
62 Actress Charlotte
64 P.O. concern

ACROSS

1 Gen. Arnold
4 Nap
8 "Blood Wedding" dramatist
13 Ailing girl in opera
14 State as fact
15 French soup favorite
16 Eager
17 Boxing's square
18 Math word
19 "____ the Wind," film classic of '61
22 Landers or Miller
23 Grant or Peggy
24 Uncooked
26 Companion of yon
29 Uninvited ones
34 Component in perfume or medicine
35 Fox or turkey follower
36 "____ a Song Go . . ."
37 Clarke and West
38 Edwin or J. Wilkes
39 Location
40 Coup d'____
41 Lhasa ____ (dog breed)
42 Bodega or boutique
43 Marks off as a poor risk
45 ____ Sea (saline lake of Calif.)
46 Suffix with persist
47 Certain weed
48 Partner of fi
51 Bacall-to-Bogart phrase
57 Ionian isle
59 Locality
60 Little ____, fictional tugboat
61 County in Ky.
62 Salacious expression
63 Monster
64 Like many curs
65 "¿Cómo ____ Vd.?"
66 Home for two peas

DOWN

1 "____ Sierra," Bogart film
2 Belonging to me: Fr.
3 Part of a slangy retort
4 Living room
5 Like campus halls
6 Word before lease
7 Therefore
8 Doone and Luft
9 "Two ____ raft" (poached eggs with toast)
10 "Rio" girl
11 Offering to a mendicant
12 Poet's soon
13 Paw's mate
20 "On Your ____," Rodgers-Hart 1936 musical
21 Anger
25 One-horse town
26 "Northeaster" painter
27 Heated
28 Tire feature
29 Kind of cut or beam
30 Newspaper pic style
31 Thomas Stearns ____
32 Prefix with grade or rocket
33 Dutch painter or British novelist
35 Constantly fail to pass the bar
38 African language
42 Garment of India
44 Harm
45 Tuaregs' region
47 Canary's statement
48 Con man's scheme
49 Musical ending
50 Bani-Sadr's homeland
52 Shopper stopper
53 "____ bien!" (Pierre's approval)
54 Takeout phrase at a diner
55 Killanin's title
56 Parisian season
58 Garden of Eden fruit

26

ACROSS

1 Route
5 Buffet dish
10 Cicatrix
14 ____ code
15 Encomium
16 Verrett specialty
17 Beautiful birds
20 Meddle
21 Far from fresh
22 Greek theater
23 French dairy product
25 Corrode
28 Word with wing or wood
29 Bird call
30 Formerly
31 Private eye
34 Walked with a certain gait
35 Prynne's stigma
38 Plymouth prisons
39 Headdresses
40 Be flirtatious
41 Dir. from Albuquerque to Denver
42 Invalid's food
45 Dijon dance
46 Proofreading mark
49 Had origin
51 Armadillo
53 Modifies
54 Sherlock Holmes story
58 Fishing need
59 Necktie
60 Feudal bigwig
61 Hand over
62 Urban illumination
63 Gaelic

DOWN

1 Parish head
2 Arched passageway
3 Joined
4 Memorable mime
5 Melampus was one
6 High in pitch
7 Batch
8 Quartz variety
9 Cotton cloth
10 Big brain
11 Belief
12 Make known
13 Ethiopian title
18 Author Deighton
19 Exist
23 Sky traveler
24 Ordinary
26 Maple-tree genus
27 Lewis or Nugent
29 Nickname in "East of Eden"
30 Stable fare
31 White ____
32 A wk. has 168 of these
33 Point of view
34 Sch. auxiliary
35 Tale of the Forsytes
36 Put together, as parts of a book
37 Sooner than, to Shakespeare
38 Tar
42 Tulip tree
43 Garden blooms
44 Crushing tool
46 Obnoxious fellow
47 Indo-European
48 Work incentive
49 Oklahoma city
50 Peep show
52 Whimper
53 Biblical book
54 Spark stream
55 ____ out (finish)
56 Sgt. or cpl.
57 Absalom, to David

27

ACROSS

1 Iridescent gem
5 Frat-party garments
10 Orlando rarity
14 Local food store, for short
15 Old-womanish
16 Fundy phenomenon
17 Flap, as a sail
18 Bogged down
19 Mucho
20 Terpsichorean two-some
23 Irks
24 Jerry Pate's turf piercer
25 Getaway
28 Noxious vapors
32 Pillage
33 O'Neill's "____ for the Misbegotten"
35 Carney or Buchwald
36 Hit film of 1933
40 "There! ____ Said It Again": Mann-Evans song
41 He spoke for Standish
42 Two-toed sloth
43 Chilean poet's family
45 Abominate
47 Nest
48 Centers
50 Sometime co-star with 20 Across
55 Becloud
56 ____-visual equipment
57 Fracas
59 On the Caspian
60 Tree lump
61 Caribbean sight
62 Servants
63 Teasdale and a Roosevelt
64 Lowly laborer

DOWN

1 "____ bodkins!"
2 Riches
3 Winglike
4 Educated class
5 Mexican dish
6 Cat-____-tails
7 Strengthens
8 Give ____ up (assist)
9 Political agitation
10 Western vehicles
11 Egyptian delta
12 Aroma
13 Moist
21 Brief swim
22 Sartre's "Nothingness"
25 Puckish
26 Find the answers
27 More bashful
28 Cut, as a lawn
29 W.W. I battle site
30 Diva's numbers
31 Chubby
33 Appends
34 One of the Three Stooges
37 Comaneci or Boulanger
38 Sunday best
39 Surpass
44 Disclose
45 Prattles foolishly
46 Poetic contraction
48 Fragrant wood
49 Prime Minister before Suzuki
50 Otherwise
51 One-on-one encounter
52 The Danube, in Hungary
53 Seine tributary
54 ____ contendere
55 Scrooge's expression
58 Decimal base

28

ACROSS

1 Geometrical figure
5 Commanded
9 Kind of water or cracker
13 Perpetually
14 ____ nut
15 Coin of Persia: 1826–1932
16 Key phrase
19 Chicago transportation
20 W.W. II correspondent ____ Pyle
21 Passage
22 Oppositionist
23 With: Prefix

24 Aurora borealis
31 Cut
32 "The youth replies, '____'": Emerson
33 Ages upon ages
34 Exchange premium
35 Turn
37 Caravel of 1492
38 Vessel on a pedestal
39 Inevitable
40 Fat: Comb. form
41 "On the ____ toe": Milton
46 Pershing's cmd.

47 Welfare
48 Heap of stones
51 Violinist Isaac
53 Deplorable
56 Hasty, superficial treatment, with "the"
59 Weaving machine
60 Source of mescal
61 Dash
62 Austria's first chartered city
63 Encyclopedia, e.g.
64 Cyrano's outstanding feature

DOWN

1 Yield
2 Ellipse
3 Intelligence
4 Sea eagle
5 Skullcap
6 Longfellow's bell town
7 Take out
8 English cathedral city
9 Winter sport
10 Corps.; assns.
11 Actress Arlene
12 Bet
14 Place to sleep
17 Transmitted
18 Store up

22 Cartoonist Peter
23 Lath
24 Pola of silent films
25 ____ to (because of)
26 Split
27 Sgt. or cpl.
28 Spyri's children's story
29 Refreshing
30 Make a sharp, cracking sound
31 Pull with force
35 Gust
36 Wolfert or Eaker
37 Kind of bank or flag: Abbr.

39 Shorthand transcriber
42 Seraglios
43 Noon or midnight
44 Mountaintop nest
45 Vocalized
48 Nursery king
49 By and by
50 Sacred image
51 State flower of Utah
52 Mine car
53 Normandy town
54 Exclamation of woe
55 Unit of force
57 Large tub
58 Brooder of a sort

ACROSS

1 Bucket
5 Arizona Indian
9 The Crimson Tide, for short
13 4,840 square yards
14 Toward the mouth
15 Disappears slowly
16 Chopsticks?
18 Beds for Leo and Elsa
19 Actress O'Shea of music-hall fame
20 Ali ____
22 Needle feature
23 Encircle
24 Part of a Warsaw bank?
26 Tweed, for one
28 Enclosure for a sandhog
29 Feign
30 "____ the Way," 1957 song
31 Mining car
34 "Shoe the horse, shoe ____"
37 Seeming intersection of earth and sky
39 Word with tooth or heart
40 "The orb of the day"
41 Antiochian or Augustan
42 Asiatic bird
44 Strikebreaker
45 Rio kook?
48 Favorite Scrooge utterance
49 Small ape
50 Saudi Arabian province
51 Oz figure
54 Revoke, as a marriage
56 Hamlet?
58 "Mortal ____," Huxley book
59 Heal
60 Italian cousin of Mount St. Helens
61 Spot for Sonny Boy
62 Annexes
63 Puma's prey

DOWN

1 NATO, for one
2 Word with tooth or heart
3 Hubbub in Dublin?
4 Opticians' products
5 Hockey great
6 Anglo-Saxon money
7 Overheat
8 Paragons
9 Barnyard sound
10 Ta-ta, in Tours
11 Streep of Hollywood
12 What you have going for you
15 Taste, to a Londoner
17 Intention
21 Illuminated
24 Homophone for 1 Across
25 Not pro
26 Casey's cudgel
27 Late protest singer
28 Trusts
32 Prague comrade?
33 Sabra's dance
35 City ENE of Paris
36 Forward passes in football
37 Sept follower
38 Collar
40 Incited
43 Riddle
44 Polished
45 Ebon or raven
46 Chattered incessantly
47 Athlete with an army
48 Fell for
51 Urchins
52 Bancroft or Boleyn
53 Intimate
55 Rubber tree
57 Word with split or tight

30

ACROSS

1 Defense force
5 December song
10 Belgrade native
14 Admirer
15 Dote on
16 Window part
17 National Park in N.M.
20 Underground worker
21 Bad actors
22 Boat on a regular route
23 Resources
25 Region of SW Morocco
26 Jane Wyatt's "Star Trek" role
28 Effective; vigorous
32 Resembling a shortening
33 Pleasure boat
34 Ethan Allen's brother
35 On the ____ (estranged)
36 Fail to follow suit: Var.
37 These come by the dozen
38 Black cuckoo
39 Biblical prophet
40 Handy specialty
41 Visionaries
43 Bob or pageboy
44 One of the Maxwells
45 French cup
46 Menu item in Mexico
49 Lots of time
50 Chop
53 Mack Sennett offering
56 ____ Alto
57 Laughing sound
58 What Vachon guards
59 Minute rock particles in water
60 Golf clubs
61 Roman calendar date

DOWN

1 Rudiments
2 Cut grain
3 Larry Hagman's mother
4 Actor Brynner
5 Beach house
6 Leader of a "Party" in 1773
7 Measures of length
8 Sea mammal
9 Child's game
10 Coined money
11 Merry adventure
12 Prince Charles' sister
13 Feature of many a suit
18 Like a garden spot
19 Cyrus or Philo
24 Aims
25 Ancient district in Asia Minor
26 "Half ____ is better . . ."
27 ____ Loa
28 Temples, to Tennyson
29 Sailing-ship décor
30 Solicited earnestly
31 Roundup gear
33 Wicker basket used in pelota
36 Poet who wrote "The Blessed Damozel"
37 "Boola, Boola" singers
39 ". . . ____ of Montezuma"
40 Jerome Hines is one
42 Proverbial site of a tempest
43 Small arches
45 Passenger fare
46 Recipe amts.
47 Late queen of Jordan
48 Street for shoppers only
49 This may follow a stimulus
51 On ____ (impatient)
52 Followers of exes
54 Suffix with bombard
55 Start of the 12th century

31

ACROSS

1 Alexander Raban Waugh
5 Inspected, Sutton style
10 Sabin's counterpart
14 Sup
15 Declaim
16 Part of HOMES
17 Indigo
18 Play a guitar
19 Zenith
20 Start of a quotation from Twain
23 Fur piece
24 Extremity
25 Beethoven opera

29 Withdrew
33 Oriental sashes
34 River in western Africa
36 Ready-to-eat food products
37 Wind direction
38 Actress Ullmann
39 Harvard's neighbor in Camb.
40 Clockmaker Thomas
42 Adjust
44 Boodle
45 He gives a guarantee
47 Home of the Maple Leafs

49 Girl of song
50 Grog base
51 End of the quotation
60 Fling
61 Winged
62 He loved an Irish lass
63 Take a long, longing look
64 Stylish business establishment
65 Repetition
66 An equal
67 100-yard dash, e.g.
68 Precious

DOWN

1 A first mate
2 Londoner's floor covering
3 City in Oklahoma
4 Indonesian island
5 Author of "The Silver Chalice"
6 Bohemian
7 Variety of chalcedony
8 Needle case
9 Greek goddess of agriculture
10 Alga
11 Waggish
12 One source of vitamin C
13 Acute

21 Peruvian coin
22 Well-known dwarf
25 Broadway choreographer
26 Author of "Hedda Gabler"
27 Assemblies
28 Ken Stabler was one
29 Face an embankment
30 Imp
31 Pen name of Mary Ann Evans
32 The same
35 Servicemen
41 Go-getter
42 Liberate

43 Swift, violent stream of water
44 Moneylender
46 Stadium sound
48 Lament
51 Word with lamb or pork
52 Small sled
53 Shield décor
54 Ukrainian, e.g.
55 Ridge
56 Institution founded by Henry VI
57 Chinese horn
58 Actress Moreno
59 Poetic negative

ACROSS

1 Knack
5 "____ Maisie Knew," James novel
9 Kind of note
13 Theater award
14 Hollandaise, e.g.
15 High: Comb. form
16 Route for Dorothy
19 Cutting tool
20 Leas
21 ____ Dame University
22 Tastes the tea
23 Also
24 Carouse

32 Bergman role in "Casablanca"
33 Chessman
34 He wrote "The College Widow"
35 Speech defect
36 One of the Allens
38 "____ star to steer her by": Masefield
39 The Buckeyes' initials
40 A pirate or a choreographer
41 Memorable Israeli leader

42 Argonauts' prize
47 Mimic
48 Holly
49 Bizarre
52 Ghanaian export
54 Chat
57 Kubrick film, with "A"
60 Edible tuber
61 Velocity
62 Sandburg or Van Doren
63 Soon
64 Thoroughly
65 Etc.'s relative

DOWN

1 Court painter to Charles III
2 Old World mountain goat
3 "The round ____" (wastepaper basket)
4 ____ Aviv
5 Indiana-Illinois boundary river
6 New Mexico artist Peter
7 "____ and Galatea," Handel opus
8 Shamus
9 Strand
10 "Little Things Mean ____," 1954 song
11 What the man of La Mancha followed
12 Pelt

14 Used a besom
17 Neglect
18 Understood
22 Cinch
23 Resembling a certain fiber
24 Guide
25 Like stout
26 Offspring
27 Final stanza of a Pindaric poem
28 Boy
29 Indian princess
30 Relating to early literature of Iceland
31 "The Wreck of the Mary ____," Innes novel
36 Sly trick
37 Singular

38 Stock-exchange heading
40 Part of a ruble
43 Waiter or servant
44 This bears an image of Monticello
45 Inundate
46 Cordelia's father
49 Eight: Comb. form
50 ____ Bator, Mongolia
51 Bullring cry, sometimes
52 Deal with successfully
53 Russian city
54 Small two-winged insect
55 Taj Mahal city
56 Dingaling thing
58 Compass pt.
59 Person who excels

33

ACROSS

1 ____ California
5 Moistens
10 W. Va. product
14 Like 2, 4, 6, 8 . . .
15 Predecessor of febrero
16 Airfield near Paris
17 Parched
18 "Anything Goes" composer
20 Meredith Willson's "76"
22 ____ nova, dance meaning "new bump"
23 Source of penicillin
24 City near Düsseldorf
26 7th, 8th, 9th, etc. in N.Y.C.
29 Secondhand transactions
33 Hell's Angel, for one
34 Fulcrum for an oar
36 Pedro's cheer
37 Juillet seasons
38 Evidence
39 Fancy follower
40 Mus. adaptation
41 Light refractor
42 Particle
43 Asian wind
45 Early films
47 Rugged rocks
49 ____ Brothers of comedic fame
50 Entree item
53 "____, Bothered and Bewildered"
57 "Mister Wonderful" star, with "Jr."
59 Circle of light
60 Hold fast
61 River to the Rhone
62 Gaelic
63 Wee drams
64 Ancient toilers
65 1, 9, 66, etc.

DOWN

1 "____ Foot Forward"
2 Declare
3 "Roberta" composer
4 Flowerlike sea animals
5 Solve, as a cipher
6 Prolific composer or author
7 Riot
8 Where printers gather
9 Dip or dunk
10 Cigar with blunt ends
11 Table scraps
12 City NNW of Nîmes
13 Heavenly Harp
19 Falstaffian
21 Smudge
25 Prefix for esteem, help, etc.
26 At right angles to the keel
27 In ____ (in glass)
28 Instrument for Bob Haggart, Slam Stewart, et al.
30 "On Your Toes" lyricist
31 Choose
32 Looks for
35 O.T. book
38 Malayan outrigger canoe
39 Beaumont's collaborator
41 Cartoon pig
42 Move swiftly
44 Rascals
46 Rainbows
48 "____ Brides for . . ."
50 N.C.O.
51 Elephant's-ear
52 Give off
54 Metal thread
55 Other
56 Female hares
58 Atlantic City cube

34

ACROSS

1 Border on
5 Port city of Iraq
10 Accepted standards
14 Stalagmite milieu
15 Modern Greek name for Greece
16 Trans-____, Russian range
17 Stravinsky's "Le Sacre du Printemps"
20 Word in a film ad
21 Kind of kitchen
22 Stassen, to Eisenhower in 1953
23 Large crucifix
25 Pass
28 Moderated
32 Ear: Comb. form
33 Item for John Sloan
34 Deity who became Tahiti's national god
35 Behave in a formal manner
39 Chariot chaser
40 Gossip
41 Date for Duclos
42 Too long, as a speech
44 Danish chess master
46 Regarding
47 Insincere statements
48 Plant fiber
51 "And the ____ stars set their watch": T. Campbell
55 S. Y. Agnon novel
58 In ____ (in position)
59 Singer Haggard
60 Churchill's foreign minister
61 Declare positively
62 Abbot's subordinate
63 Lillums Lovewell's beau

DOWN

1 New Testament book
2 Thai money
3 Eye part
4 Diamondback inhabiting a salt marsh
5 Happen (to)
6 Coeur d'____, Idaho
7 Plod in paludous places
8 Brit. air arm
9 ". . . egregiously an ____": Iago
10 Ostentation
11 Came down to terra firma
12 Romany wife
13 Index
18 Georgia O'Keeffe's "Black ____"
19 Streisand hit song
23 Adjust an alarm clock
24 Henri Philippe Benoni ____ Joseph Pétain
25 Let up
26 Minstrel
27 Palm cockatoo of Australia
28 Unexpressed but implied
29 Studies
30 The Cubs banked on him for years
31 Ranking member of a group
33 Provide, as with talents
36 California mountain pass
37 ____ about (approximately)
38 Strict French general: 17th century
43 He straightened up and flew right
44 Fierce piercer on a steed
45 B'way org.
47 Instrument for Yo-Yo Ma
48 Words before boy or girl
49 Weapon for Mack the Knife
50 Place for a chapeau
51 Kálmán operetta
52 Knot
53 Fleuret's kin
54 Redgrave or Fontanne
56 Deviling
57 Lehár's "____ Rastelbinder"

35

ACROSS

1 LL.B.
4 Items in a Hall of Fame
9 W.W. I plane
13 Stern, to Scotty
15 Houston athlete
16 Forbidden
17 Stringed instrument
18 Slow-moving
20 Jot
21 Emulate Magellan
22 Bass viols
26 Corundum
27 One of Santa's eight
32 Half a dance
34 Painter of waterlilies
37 Name meaning "sweet or pleasant"
38 Ripening agent
40 Approaches
42 Proper's partner
43 Santa ____, city in Uruguay
45 Dear
47 Between Sault and Marie
48 Asian delta
50 Up ____ (stumped)
52 Deteriorate
57 Shocked
61 "Once ____ a time . . ."
62 What cold or fear causes
65 Give up
66 Razorbills
67 Run away
68 Gardner of whodunits
69 Editor's notation
70 Yawps
71 Scottish seaport

DOWN

1 Off the cuff
2 "Happy birthday ____"
3 Sweater type
4 ____-relief
5 J.F.K.'s service
6 Tolerate
7 Test
8 Filled in a c.w.p.
9 Single
10 S.A. rodent
11 Help in heinous activities
12 Fop
14 Kingdom
19 Tower-city native
23 Opp. of masculine
24 Press
25 Force units
28 Fool
29 Western
30 Utter
31 Hoarfrost
32 Soothe
33 Chill
35 End a certain strike
36 Trick's alternative
39 ____ Grande
41 Third son of Adam
44 Acute or obtuse item
46 Prefix with mature
49 Johnny Miller is one
51 Elicit
53 "I cannot ____ lie"
54 Famous French theater
55 Divine
56 Scoff
57 Moslem titles
58 Unhappy look
59 Sack or bag
60 Helper: Abbr.
63 N.Y.C. is one
64 Berlin's "____ a Rag Picker"

36

ACROSS

1 Laundry
5 Kind of circus
9 Grand or little ____
13 Recorded proceedings
14 Signified
15 Marco ____
16 Precariously
19 Kind of dance or party
20 View from Bogotá
21 S. California city
22 Pump or gillie
23 Part of U.K.
24 Skipper's command

31 Two-legged wolf's look
32 Rolling; undulate
33 Word before hooray
35 Rivaling: Prefix
36 White with age
38 Provide a feast for
39 Before VWX
40 Hindu woman's garment
41 Kelp
42 Generosity
47 Chaney or Nol
48 Concept

49 Cavalier poet Thomas ____
52 Siouan of Oklahoma
54 By way of
57 Clumsy person's problem
60 Composer of "Rule, Britannia"
61 Mount
62 Landed
63 White-flecked horse
64 Book by Oates
65 Ferber or Best

DOWN

1 Transport buoyantly
2 43,560 square feet
3 Ancient Greek portico
4 Noah's second son
5 Parried, with "off"
6 Carry into a carrier
7 Tolkien creatures
8 From ____ Z
9 Parasite
10 Clamorous
11 High: Comb. form
12 Hawaiian honey eater
14 Massenet opera
17 Guffaw
18 Mork's friend on TV
22 Title of respect in India
23 Jealousy's next of kin

24 Exclamation of concern
25 Slowly, to Serkin
26 Slackening; abatement
27 Belle's boy
28 Row
29 Neighbor of Peru
30 Kansas City's N.B.A. team
34 Items in some patches
36 Author of "Look Who's Talking!"
37 "Are you a man ____ mouse?"
38 Actor Andrews
40 Pure; spotless
43 The Cosmos, e.g.
44 Crown

45 Bordered
46 Exploit
49 Trout type
50 Prefix with space
51 Indian prince
52 Formal affirmation
53 Large knife of yore
54 Grassland of South Africa
55 ". . . pudding ____ the eating"
56 Fox terrier of films from 1934 to 1947
58 Conferee at Potsdam in '45
59 Tartan wearer's turn-down

37

ACROSS

1 Clerical vestments
5 ____ père ou fils
10 Fellow
14 Tabby talk
15 Pointless
16 Aura
17 Herman or George Herman
18 Portents for Pompey
19 "____ Your Face Before Me," 1937 song
20 Diabolic
22 Algonquian gelt
24 Jackets
25 Most ashen
26 He "hit 'em where they ain't"
29 Sacred
30 States of health, prosperity, etc.
34 Gobbled
35 Mixes
37 Ordinal-number ender
38 26-inning game, e.g.
41 Modern hairdo
42 St. Louis Browns Hall of Famer
46 Like a bright night
48 Brooklyn's "Kentucky Colonel"
49 Run the 100
50 Epithet for Napoleon, with "the"
53 ____ Man McGinnity
54 Cremonan violinmaker
56 French battle site in W.W. II
57 Catches
58 Magic maker
59 Labor
60 Cozy spot
61 Veeps, mgrs., etc.
62 Sp. miss

DOWN

1 Prefix with dextrous
2 Slender
3 "Rapid Robert" of no-hit fame
4 In a very nice way
5 Canadian quints' name
6 Reveal
7 Junk or fan follower
8 Massachusetts cape
9 Shoreline protectors
10 Foolish fancy
11 Metal straps
12 Alaskan native
13 Cowper creation
21 Louis XIV was one
23 "A" to Moishe
25 Earl or Duke
26 Sound of a solid hit
27 Jot
28 Buck ____, baseball Hall of Famer
31 Type of telescope
32 Antoine's "to be"
33 Memorable baseball-mad restaurateur
35 Deficit
36 Royalist of '76
39 Versus
40 Lottery prize
41 "A" on box scores
43 Amatory
44 World ____
45 Plural endings
46 Binge
47 Meadowlands events
49 Coach-to-batter gesture
50 Malacca
51 Landed
52 Piano theme song for Vincent Lopez
55 "Super ____" (Lee Trevino)

38

ACROSS

1 Kind of hopper
5 Actress Verdon
9 First word in a Dostoyevsky title
14 Whole: Comb. form
15 A cardinal's is red
16 Ishmael's mother
17 Times of decision
19 "____ by any other name . . .": Juliet
20 Novel by 39 Down
21 Domestication is their vocation
23 Unusual individuals
25 Apr. and Aug.
26 Bags
29 Madison and Montgomery, e.g.
34 Like apples ready to bake
35 Some go a long distance
36 Shipment from India
37 Dry as dust
38 Arroyo
39 Shirley Verrett, for one
40 Marseille Mrs.
41 Reclines indolently
42 Wandering one
43 Historic site in Texas (first battle of Mexican War)
45 Meshy pattern
46 Mailman's tour: Abbr.
47 Intertwine
49 Bluebeard's curious wife
52 Speaks sonorously
56 Part of a pasha's palace
57 Atomic particles
59 Maxim's cousin
60 Hold a horse back until the homestretch
61 Be remiss about
62 Of somatic tissue
63 Attar asset
64 Puts together

DOWN

1 Mother of Chastity
2 She gets what she wants
3 Couturier Cassini
4 Altered, as evidence
5 Actress Tammy
6 Ardent one
7 Helmsman's abbr.
8 Abode in a roble
9 Goatlike antelope
10 Most exceptional
11 Composer Stravinsky
12 What a priest says
13 Prior to, to Prior
18 Like a runcible spoon
22 Antonym of meagerly
24 Shore-dinner tidbit
26 Impish one
27 Bellini opera
28 Rebel angel in "Paradise Lost"
30 Start of a Shakespearean title
31 Kicking's sidekick
32 Rod often seen on a court
33 Causing goose flesh
35 James Dean fans, e.g.
38 Robot in Hebrew folklore
39 Author of "Loon Lake"
41 Martyred opponent of Mary I
42 John of "Carousel" fame
44 Spanish philosopher ____ y Gasset
45 Cavalryman of a sort
48 Stop the engines at sea
49 Meet the bet at Reno
50 Body fed by the Amu Darya
51 Baltic island
53 One place where you seldom bake in Alaska
54 City in Oklahoma
55 Stratosphere streakers, for short
56 Something to fling into a ring
58 Aladdin, e.g.

39

ACROSS

1 These make flights
7 Cheekiness
12 Goes rapidly
14 Flayed
16 Nero's first wife
17 Name on a silver dollar
18 Ebro, for one
19 Joins
21 Spread
22 Raison d'____
24 Water bird
25 Info
26 "Plaza ____," Simon play
28 "____ M," Christie novel
29 Zoo equipment
30 Symbol of aridity
32 "Least said, ____ mended"
34 Prefix with bar or bath
35 Grimalkin
36 Fanciful notion
40 Mussulman
43 Flawless
44 "Te ____," Ovidian valentine
46 Of tissue
48 What brevity is to wit
49 Frugal
51 This comes before tat
52 Sleeper, e.g.
53 Canton residents
55 Year in Leif Ericsson's era
56 He wrote "The Last Hurrah"
58 Item served with soup
60 Five Nations group
61 Moppet's vehicle
62 Be displeasing to
63 Arikara abodes

DOWN

1 Props
2 Roman historian
3 W. Irving work
4 Give ____ try
5 Intensifies, with "up"
6 Bog bird
7 Goof
8 Pshaw!
9 Hardwood
10 Cold ____
11 Roman councils
13 City in central Kansas
14 Foyt, Unser et al.
15 Hereditary ruler
20 Pledge to the preacher
23 Morally right
25 Misused participle
27 Canvas support
29 Take it easy
31 Louis Philippe, for one
33 Exclamation
36 Lake herrings
37 Roman Empire conqueror
38 Nerve cell
39 Tropical American animals
40 Fen
41 Babylonian's neighbor
42 Broadway event
45 His wife was in the Gang of Four
47 Their words are absurd
49 Mass of bass
50 What legislatures do
53 Formerly
54 Plumlike fruit
57 Little knot
59 Plaything

40

ACROSS

1 Kind of can or tray
4 X-____
9 Slammer occupant
12 Cambodian coin
14 Slip away surreptitiously
15 ". . . and behold a ____ horse": Rev. 6:8
16 Fronton term
17 Logomachy
19 Island east of Sumatra
21 Like oxygen
22 ____ incognita
24 Estrada of "CHiPs"
25 Dempsey or Louis specialty
28 Stockades in Russia
32 Gluck et al.
33 Past or present
35 Kind of sch.
36 Anna or a gun
37 Gold casting
38 Gaucho's gait
39 Kind of lion or cow
40 "For want of ____ the shoe . . ."
41 Senior
42 More ____ (approximately)
44 Hygienic
46 Suffix with comment
48 Farrell's "A World I ____ Made"
49 Helical
53 Málaga lady
56 Final chance
58 Leather, in Lyon
59 River in Tuscany
60 Del ____, county in Calif.
61 Within: Comb. form
62 Sodden
63 Fall fabric
64 Morning mist

DOWN

1 Sadat is one
2 Storage place for missiles
3 Substantial repast
4 Change, as a novel
5 Between Miss. and Ga.
6 Bullring target
7 Poetic form used by Horace
8 Inventor Lee ____
9 Aid acronym
10 Automotive pioneer
11 Monster's loch
13 Telephone installer
15 Welk rendition
18 ____-in vote
20 Alexandrian and Babylonian
23 Mount St. Helens's counterpart in Sicily
25 Signe of Sweden
26 Modify
27 Toomey of movies
29 Philander
30 Loom bar
31 Unemotional
34 E. E. Hale antihero
37 Overbearing
38 Power
40 "When You Wish Upon ____": 1940 song
41 Swan follower
43 Keep an ____ the ground
45 Hunted for hornbills' homes
47 Plant anew
49 Side dish
50 Father of modern surgery
51 "____ It Romantic?": 1932 song
52 Containing gold
54 Costain's "____ with Me"
55 In a line
57 Map abbr.

41

ACROSS

1 Tight grip
6 Relative of drat
10 A-one
14 Palatial
15 On and on
16 Composer Satie
17 Masqat citizen
18 Inference or deduction
20 Sport
21 Arias for tenors
23 Mrs. ____ Warfield Simpson
24 Sheerness
27 Side
28 Oak genus
32 Former ruler of Iran
35 Two-pointer made with ease
37 Tolerable
38 "Black gold"
39 Cha or bohea
40 ____ room
41 Erect
43 Factotum
45 Roll top
46 Not so prolix
48 Grade of a U.S.N. enlisted man
50 Court disaster
55 On ____ (broadcasting)
58 Teen-____
59 Nope
60 Rare things
62 "The Man ____"
64 ____ were
65 Source of some grease
66 Mopish one
67 Bankrolls
68 "H.M.S. Pinafore" group
69 Went through

DOWN

1 Tenant's farm
2 Loris
3 Guam's capital
4 Staff
5 Crinkly fabric
6 Rhetorical
7 To have: Fr.
8 Saul's grandfather or uncle
9 Adult
10 People often behind bars
11 Viva-voce
12 ____ Thomas, author of "Down These Mean Streets"
13 "The ____ the limit!"
19 Cluny product
22 Fire____, semi-precious stone
25 Unspecified degree
26 NOW cause
29 Pith
30 Wields
31 Clout
32 Rowan tree
33 Yesterday, in Metz
34 "Merry" in a game name
36 Indeed
42 Meals
43 Bride, to the groom
44 Delayed
45 Syn., for one
47 Pass quickly
49 Rose nuisance
51 Sprinkle
52 Hole-____
53 Cleft
54 Try hard
55 Unfreeze
56 "For ____ jolly . . ."
57 Bagnold
61 The U.S., in France
63 Pitcher part

42

ACROSS

1 Weight allowance
5 Fen plant
9 Surrealist painter
13 Persian poet
14 Drying device
15 Hodgepodge
16 Hopper was one
19 Slanders
20 Santa ____ Race Track
21 Poetic contraction
22 Get along
24 Rejects with contempt
28 Fine fur
29 Fruit seed
32 Siberian stream
33 ____ Island, Canada
34 Epoch
35 William Allen White was one
39 Corrode
40 Dwarfish
41 National League team
42 Work busily
43 Black
44 Turned over
46 Payments to psychiatrists
47 O.T. book
48 City NW of Genoa
51 Lake Michigan port and resort
56 Grantland Rice et al.
59 Tiny bit
60 Poet who married Thomas Mann's daughter
61 Eagerly expectant
62 Ancient city
63 Strip
64 Disown

DOWN

1 Clothing for Cassius
2 Disney's inventive mouse
3 Carpentry tool
4 Gaelic
5 Kitchen utensil
6 Olympian lad
7 Wriggly swimmer
8 Actress Joanne
9 Metaphysical poet
10 Others, to Ovid
11 Register
12 Greek letter
14 Church sections
17 Shipment to Pittsburgh
18 "Little Miss ____," Shirley Temple film
22 Derby entry
23 Again
24 Rest
25 Cycle
26 Singleness
27 Sinking ship's deserter
28 Having substance
29 ____ four (small cake)
30 ". . . Alice Blue Gown" musical
31 Reduced
33 Showy flowers
36 Global area
37 Old Norse poem
38 Tourist haven
44 Church law
45 Eastern notable
46 Terra ____
47 Garment part
48 Autocrat
49 ____ snuff (satisfactory)
50 Follower of ball or sun
51 Ancient Asian
52 South African native village
53 Cécile's cranium
54 Where Tralee is
55 Spot
57 A sugar source
58 ____ anemone (perennial plant)

43

ACROSS

1 Playwright Connelly: 1890–1981
5 Passport stamp
9 Impertinent
14 Cupid
15 Enrages
16 Fine coffee
17 Type of pasta
19 Mistake
20 Foes
21 Gloomy planet
22 Printing measures
23 Petty tyrant
25 Van Druten's "____ a Camera"
28 Maternity-ward announcement
30 Dos Passos trilogy
33 Reject
35 High-school dance
36 Winged
37 Type of pasta
39 Type of pasta
41 "____ homo!"
42 Smell ____ (suspect)
44 Divert
45 British collation
46 Keep going despite difficulties
48 ____ volatile
49 Brave ones
51 Sibling's nickname
53 Playground adjuncts
55 Mussolini was one
59 Strops
60 Type of pasta
62 Useless
63 Quaggy ground
64 Dickens girl
65 Sauce for pasta
66 Bronze and Stone
67 Gait

DOWN

1 Nutmeg
2 "I met ____ . . ."
3 Lariat or riata
4 Word with de menthe
5 Most hideous
6 Eye part
7 Japanese coin
8 Faulkner's "____ Lay Dying"
9 Bedaubed
10 Heart connection
11 Honest or careful
12 Restaurateur Toots
13 Tale
18 Coat or cloud interior
21 Plant opening
23 Patriotic org.
24 Scraps, NASA style
25 Ait
26 Rapidly
27 Large, musky grapes
29 Less obese
31 Tomato sauce for pasta
32 Shakespearean sprite
34 "Norma ____," 1979 film
36 Goal
38 Nostrils
40 Disappear
43 Fool
46 Magician's word
47 Oranges or Indians
50 Skilled
52 Odor
53 The Andrea Doria was one
54 Solitary
55 High cost of leaving
56 Roman road
57 French town on the Vire
58 Pinball term
60 Like many a bairn
61 Greedy one

44

ACROSS

1 Eloper with a spoon
5 One of Nero Wolfe's employees
9 "Dracula," e.g.
14 Division term
15 Steak order
16 Soothsayer
17 Jelly ingredient
18 Actress Raines
19 Kingdom
20 Sayers sleuth
23 Prepare to drive
24 Chinese: Prefix
25 Bread and whisky
28 The right to go out
32 Basis for a whodunit
36 Biggers hero
38 Handshake
39 Variety show
40 Johnny ____
41 Special police squad
42 Jewish month
43 Hoodwink
44 Adjust again
45 Miracle
47 Vega's constellation
49 Gabor and Tanguay
51 Dolts
55 Late master of suspense
61 Evita
62 Where Baghdad is
63 Aweather's opposite
64 Charteris creation, with "The"
65 This might be Erie
66 Marine fish
67 Kefauver
68 Old English court
69 Parts of "Arsenic and Old Lace"

DOWN

1 It's on the watch
2 Gold bar
3 Gaze
4 Batu Khan's Golden ____
5 Like a ghost story
6 Sentry's order
7 A first name in whodunit lore
8 Dreads
9 Intrepid
10 Scene of a Poe mystery
11 Turkish dignitaries
12 Lounging slipper
13 Kind of ant or worm
21 Strained serving
22 Vienna, to the Viennese
26 Tan color
27 Pom-pom ammunition
29 White-tailed divers for fish
30 Six, in old dice games
31 What X marks
32 Crow's crop
33 Put up new wallpaper
34 ____ Skavinsky Skavar
35 A homicide, in police parlance
37 With skill
41 Impudent
43 Alum
46 Happenings
48 Mobster's business
50 Con man's decoy
52 Milan's Met, with "La"
53 Greek dialect
54 Hound's trail
55 Church feature
56 Meadows
57 Glass ingredient
58 Dies ____
59 Victimize
60 Beer barrels

45

ACROSS

1 N'Djamena is its capital
5 ____ with (experienced)
10 Hopped a plane
14 ____ Rud, river on Afghanistan's boundary
15 Man of Masqat
16 "Damn Yankees" gal
17 Don Juan's mother
18 Uris novel
19 Gooey or gluey
20 Newspaper
22 Clowns
24 Not busy
25 "Wozzeck" composer
26 Alter
29 Effluvium
30 Like Mary Quant's style
33 "Roots" author
34 Coal source
36 Spring bloomer
37 Luigi's mail
38 Of a period
39 Exigencies
41 Actor-musician Nelson
42 Def., maybe
43 Pound
44 Oz V.I.P.
45 Unclear
46 Actress Louise
47 Raucous cry
50 Coiffure tuft
53 Influence
54 "The Man ____," 1924 song
56 Romantic interlude
58 Article for Hans
59 Arch-consumerist
60 Slangy turndown
61 Dictator
62 Coarse
63 An Olympian

DOWN

1 Greek letter
2 Put up drapes
3 Environs
4 Vertigo
5 Blotch
6 Ham it up
7 Finish line
8 "____ voce poco far," Rossini aria
9 Fast-food place
10 Cast
11 Places
12 Actress Sommer
13 Methods
21 Nervous
23 Not care ____
25 Lancaster et al.
26 Golf shots
27 Bandleader James
28 Sci-fi heavy
29 Confused
30 Persian prince's title
31 Walking ____ (elated)
32 X-ed
34 Rueful
35 Theater area
37 Enigmatic
40 Close tightly
41 Piggery sound
44 Car attachments
45 Czech coin
46 Jabberwocky word
47 Blueprint datum, for short
48 Cross-examine
49 Bone attached to a ginglymus
50 Rowdydow
51 What anosmic people do not sense
52 Erratum
55 Gibbon
57 Author Whitten

46

ACROSS

1 Finishing nail
5 Disguised prince
9 Kind of cherry or chestnut
14 Rich material
15 Regan's father
16 Epicure, e.g.
17 Ancient coin
18 Family that lost Modena in 1803
19 Beldame
20 Reprimand
23 Fives and nines, e.g.
24 Miami's county
25 Of flying: Prefix
28 Landlord's income
32 Israel's first ambassador to U.S.
36 Result of a hole in a molar
38 Volume
39 Write a malicious, destructive critique
42 Awful
43 Señor, in Stuttgart
44 Dull; slow
45 Small opening, as on a cactus
47 Merit
49 Baff the golf ball
51 Guam's capital
55 Censures
61 Get up
62 He wrote "Metamorphoses"
63 Monk parrot
64 Kind of house
65 City of Seven Hills
66 V.I.P. at Kabul
67 Writer Terkel
68 ____ Islands (part of the Aleutians)
69 Left or right, e.g.

DOWN

1 Political alliance
2 City on the Bou Regreg
3 Soap plant
4 Reese or Street
5 Cut blubber from a whale
6 Advice to an energumen
7 Curser's mouthing
8 One cause of corruption
9 1971–80, e.g.
10 City in Ga. or Mo.
11 On
12 Coty or Clair
13 Worry
21 ____ Beach, of D-day fame
22 Proofreader's mark
26 Foot or potato follower
27 Pigment for Opie
29 Soliloquy starter
30 Cupid
31 Period after Mardi Gras
32 Norse heroic song
33 European dormouse
34 Alpine stream
35 Emerald Isle
37 Juno's Greek counterpart
40 Illegal lifting
41 Chauvinist
46 Proverbial weepers
48 Jim Plunkett was one
50 Rose's seamy side
52 Great burden-bearer
53 Elimelech's wife
54 Biting
55 Eleven in L.A.
56 He was: Lat.
57 Aborigine of Japan
58 "Whoopee!" in Pan's parties
59 Hudson heroine
60 Sped

47

ACROSS

1 Smith and Hirt
4 Word with side or hog
8 ____ Nostra
12 Twist
13 Prefix with liminal or national
14 River in England
15 Munich's river
16 Sorcery
18 Tiny amounts
20 Rand's "____ Shrugged"
21 Sins
22 Yawn
24 Exposed
27 Staubach threw these
31 Sew loosely
32 Straight-edged ____
33 Eerie flier
34 Superlative suffixes
35 Seraglio
36 Had on
37 Lunched
38 Vacuums
39 Freeway sign
40 Revolutionary War mercenaries
42 Post office employee
43 All ____ (eager to hear)
44 Pump, e.g.
45 Of the air
48 Sci-fi flick
52 Author of "Dracula"
55 Spread on rye
56 In one's birthday suit
57 Old-womanish
58 Take charge
59 King or Arkin
60 Persian's neighbor
61 T-man, for one

DOWN

1 In addition
2 Hilo feast
3 These got in Medusa's hair
4 Parthenon and Colosseum, e.g.
5 Chooses
6 Curve
7 Dit's companion
8 Nick of fiction
9 Ellipsoidal
10 Lounge
11 Pismires
12 Little girl's nickname
13 Excalibur was one
17 Prance
19 Algonquian
22 Intent looks
23 Particle
24 Haitian voodoo
25 Adhesive
26 Kefauver
27 Garnishes, in a way
28 Cancel a missile launch
29 Outsize
30 Guide
32 Showers
35 Kind of frost
36 Lycanthrope
38 Small vessels
39 Person of Arab-Berber descent
41 Mates, pursers et al.
42 Portion
44 Stone slab
45 ____ Eban of Israel
46 Russian river
47 ____ avis
48 Slide
49 Away from the wind
50 Scan
51 Turf
53 Headgear with kilts
54 Unit

48

ACROSS

1 "A door is not a door when it's ____"
5 Pamphleteer of '76
9 Alaskan cape
13 Accustom
14 Goad
15 Dies ____
16 Pavlovian response
18 Umpire's decision
19 Witch bird
20 She wrote "The Ponder Heart"
22 ____-surface missile
24 Lizzie's antecedent
25 Core: Comb. form
27 Elsa of literature
31 Sackcloth's partner
32 Buffalo hockey pro
33 City in Paraguay
35 Rue de la ____
36 Location of 35 Across
37 Pollution problem
38 C.I.O.'s partner
39 Restricted, as a neighborhood
40 One of Ma Bell's brood
41 Looks up to
43 Spanish laborers
44 Toronto's prov.
45 Emulate Cicero
46 He wrote "The Wapshot Chronicle"
51 Dan Beard's org.
54 By any chance
55 Solemn sagacity
57 Dasheen
58 Containing much air, as fuel
59 Ghana's capital
60 Type of gin
61 Lough ____, Ireland
62 Chinese answer to skillets

DOWN

1 Giant panda in Moscow's zoo
2 Famed cordon bleu
3 Late Gk. shipping magnate
4 Idolizes
5 Beat
6 Ramsey Lewis ____
7 Plane designer Sikorsky
8 Eagleton and two Byrds
9 Christian creed
10 ____ Roberts U., Tulsa
11 Type of vinegar
12 Hard to hold
13 "Man ____ prisoner": Plato
17 De Soto or Hudson
21 Le Montrachet, e.g.
23 Holly
25 Glove leather
26 Colo. Springs campus
27 Tutelary gods
28 Ditto: Abbr.
29 Colleague of 2 Down
30 Pelt, in a way
32 Of sound mind
34 Jaques' septet
36 Ship's window
37 Bar measurement
39 Alloy ingredient
40 Southern shrub
42 Madison's successor
43 Chief exec.
45 Sheeplike
46 Kennedy comers and goers
47 Diamond category
48 Paragon
49 Pitcher
50 Dash
52 Russia and Latvia were two: Abbr.
53 ____ rule (generally)
56 Sgt., for one

49

ACROSS

1 Sort of a sortie
5 Thurber's "The Owl in the ____"
10 Interlocution
14 ____ spumante
15 Gandhi's garb
16 Turkish liqueur
17 With 52 Across, a critical review
20 Swoons
21 Flick
22 Scold
23 Undiluted
24 Men carrying symbols of authority
27 Willie Loman, e.g.
31 Adjective for ants and aphids
32 Cremona creation, for short
33 Basil ____, noted painter of birds
34 An early invader of Britain
35 Filmy
36 Target of Mariner IV
37 Opposite of odi
38 Ring
39 "What ____ how fair she be?": G. Wither
40 Winds that mean "seasons" in Arabic
42 Kind of "Game" that hit N.Y.C. in 1954
43 Spot for a certain queen
44 Gleason's "And away ____!"
45 Cash-register recording
48 Former capital of the Mountain State
52 See 17 Across
54 Bread; dough; moola
55 Rousseau classic
56 Sonny in "The Godfather"
57 Conductor of the San Diego Symphony Orchestra
58 Acted like Hotspur
59 Trivium and quadrivium

DOWN

1 Exclamation in a Schulz comic
2 Pale as a ghost
3 Take ____ stride
4 Unrelated
5 Takes as one's own
6 Rubens's "____ Graces"
7 Rocky formations
8 Robert of "Quincy"
9 Like Arthur's Table
10 Grimalkins
11 "We ____ met the enemy . . ."
12 Actor Tamiroff: 1899–1972
13 "____ Yellow Ribbon . . ."
18 Viscount Templewood
19 Snagged in a bog
23 Porter's "You Don't Know ____": 1929
24 "____, I'm Adam"
25 Cottonwood
26 Criterion
27 Sheppard-Turpin guns
28 O'Connor's cook on TV
29 Pertinent, to a prosecutor
30 Ending with Poly and Indo
32 Glowed
35 Freshwater duck
36 Variety of Italian pottery
38 Doughboy's French ally
39 Athlete like O'Neal
41 Brokers' concerns
42 Became a sidewalk super-intendent
44 Totality
45 Winged statue in the Louvre
46 Glacial ridges
47 Historic town in Normandy
48 Zachary Taylor was one
49 Cousin of an H beam
50 Cartographer's abbr.
51 Roman family group
53 Singer Sumac

50

ACROSS

1 Scrape roughly
5 Father of The Seven Sisters
10 Brief brouhaha
14 Feel sympathy for
15 Like some eyes
16 Part of a harrow
17 Sound heard in a clowder
18 Prowl hungrily
19 Quondam
20 Tableau
22 Quercine
23 Tide not likely to cause a flood
24 Beside
27 Part of a Presidential appeal
29 Degree for an English prof.
30 Abecedarian three-some
33 Rods for roasts
34 Tom's follies
35 Second consonant
36 Tunny containers
37 Outsize
38 Dessert for a court jester?
39 Cardiologist's clue
40 Questionable
41 Filmdom family name
42 Gun one's engine
43 Piedmontese wine city
44 Baffles
45 Seat (second spelling)
47 Music-minded Renaissance priest
48 Skedaddle
50 A Lovelace lass
53 Pickerelweed
54 Samba's cousin
56 Nickname for Archibald of basketball fame
58 "Kane and ____," Jeffrey Archer novel
59 Village smithy
60 First-rate
61 Stumps
62 Sword for Lord Raglan
63 Nucleic acids, for short

DOWN

1 The least bit, infor-mally
2 "We'll tak' ____ . . .": Burns
3 Wallflower
4 Certain bonds, securities, etc.
5 Sudden
6 Toot
7 Alec Guinness and cohorts
8 Frappe base, perhaps
9 Prefix with thesis or chronic
10 Weasel prized for its fur
11 Hale-and-hearty state
12 Suffix with appear or clear
13 Owner of Leapin' Lena
21 Kit Carson's house is here
22 Baseball's Ed and Mel
25 Lament
26 Aztec god of sowing
27 Goldenrod's cousin
28 Kind of heel
31 Crystal-bearing nodule of stone
32 "Oh, woe!," in Bor-deaux
34 Cannelloni, e.g.
37 Roster
38 Adjective for a general or admiral
40 "April Morning" au-thor
41 Dog's bane
44 Plea to Pavarotti
46 Carols
48 Bridegroom's fete
49 Cheese chunk
51 Over, in Oberhausen
52 Grandma Moses
54 Preliminary papers: Abbr.
55 Eureka!
57 Something "she didn't say"

ACROSS

1 Culinary conglomeration
5 Indian state
10 Additions to ltrs.
13 Moslem deity
15 Its capital is Valletta
16 Inlet
17 Dough
18 Violently
19 Pt. or qt.
20 Time period
21 Steno's words of rejection?
23 Repeatedly, to Milton
25 Kind of neckline
26 River to the Ubangi
27 Phrase for a touring stripper?
31 Ancient, in poesy
32 Exist
33 Actor Mischa
34 Hosp. group
35 A sail
37 Acts properly
41 Suffix with musket
42 Disburden
43 Lunched
44 This may be hard to swallow
47 Like a happy medium?
49 Ship with a golden cargo
50 Suburb of Liége
51 _____ Anne de Beaupré
52 Substitute dentist's activity?
55 "_____, thou art sick!": Blake
59 Summer, to Zola
60 Lovable marsupial
61 German pronoun
62 Painter _____ Borch
63 Ethyl acetate
64 Auld Clootie, in Dundee
65 Parts of a cen.
66 Unkempt
67 Erudition

DOWN

1 Some actors
2 Unbalanced
3 _____-eyed
4 Shout on the hunt
5 To _____ (without exception)
6 Rasputin's tea maker
7 Due to appear
8 Once upon _____
9 Lots
10 Petitioned
11 Unaffected
12 Lining fabric
14 Like a kooky cook?
22 Golden Hurricanes' home
24 More faithful
27 Lived
28 Humorist Bill _____: 1826–1903
29 Yellow or Black
30 "_____ the land . . ."
31 Like an alert ballerina?
34 Naps
36 Unsaturated alcohol
37 Mary's pet's sound
38 Vacation vehicle
39 Catchall abbr.
40 Diocese
42 Stored grain
44 Kind of belt
45 Gide, e.g.
46 Girl watchers
47 Opening for molten metal
48 TV device
50 Win by _____
53 Iconoscopes, for short
54 Dogpatch negative
56 Aware of
57 Cooking direction
58 Lake in Ireland

52

ACROSS

1 Kind of cat
4 Item on a guitar
8 Eaten away
13 Gemstone
15 Città Eterna
16 Boundary
17 Marcello's wish on Jan. 1
20 Designed
21 Slangy refusal
22 Attachment on property
23 Tall tales
24 Grangers' measures
26 Teamster's rig
28 Approached
33 Lily's relative
37 Tears
39 Montélimar's river
40 Spectacle in Philadelphia on Jan. 1
43 Walking _____ (ecstatic)
44 Guy on a ship
45 Luxuriate on the beach
46 Town NNE of Paris
48 Desserts
50 Mattress-stuffing material
52 Kefauver
57 Fleming and Hunter
61 Martini base
62 Existent but unrevealed
63 "I do _____ . . ." (words for Jan. 1)
66 Dunne from Louisville
67 Certain crosses
68 Farm implement
69 British motorists' needs
70 Point on the Isle of Man
71 Method: Abbr.

DOWN

1 Chewy candy
2 "Ernani," e.g.
3 Of the cheekbone
4 Lynn of baseball
5 Sinbad's mount
6 Jan. 1, 1863
7 S.A. beast
8 Olden days
9 100 dinars
10 All: Comb. form
11 Trigonometric function
12 Kind of collar
14 Describe
18 Luck, in Ireland
19 Some bovids
24 Out of order
25 One of the Yugoslavs
27 Fail, humanly
29 Ishmael's skipper
30 Author Jaffe
31 Purposes
32 Stand in an orchestra
33 Biblical prophet
34 Object shaped like a half moon
35 Arabia's Gulf of _____
36 Actor Jannings
38 Tiffin's cousin
41 Actor Rhodes
42 Indigo is one
47 Story of heroism
49 Coral and Red
51 Niña companion
53 Street sign
54 Narrates
55 Government agent
56 Olla-podrida, etc.
57 "_____ a bird?"
58 Crooked
59 Poetic contraction
60 Sound
62 _____-majesté
64 Thing, in law
65 Capek drama

53

ACROSS

1 Cuts down
5 Venous fluid of the gods
10 Hounds
14 Square's length times width
15 Orifice
16 "Typee" sequel
17 Coat superficially
18 Noted Abstract Expressionist
20 The Vltava, to a Berliner
22 Place apart
23 Liquid used in dyes
25 Divagate
26 Greek sea god
28 Met mezzo-soprano
32 Furious
34 Firm
36 _____ Duarte Perón
37 Large containers
38 Baby's bellyache
39 Wax imprint
40 W.W. II area
41 Pitcher Ryan
42 Château-Thierry's river
43 Agree
45 Esteem
47 Yorkshire river
49 Hung up the receiver: Brit.
52 Topple
56 Mouse, for example
57 Source
59 _____ precedent
60 French composer
61 Of musical sound quality
62 Cut
63 Brings to court
64 Candidate list
65 Famous name in motordom

DOWN

1 Source of igneous rock
2 Apollo 16 lunar lander
3 The Iron Duke
4 They supply horsemen
5 Exempt from harm
6 Cote sound
7 Hovels
8 Further
9 Grandiloquent language
10 Uses a divining rod
11 Buddhist sacred mountain
12 Olympic top award
13 Lone
19 Uttered inanities
21 Light
24 Antiseptic solution
27 Type of energy
29 Worthless one
30 Karamazov brother
31 Borecole
32 With, in Nice
33 Acronym for a defense group
35 A cosmetic
38 Debases
39 A North Atlantic sea
41 Parisian nights
42 Horace or Thomas
44 Verdi's "Don _____"
46 Group of geese
48 Flynn of films
50 Malodorous
51 College socs.
52 Temple team
53 Offspring of a vache
54 French women's magazine
55 Jazz singer Simone
58 Cole or Turner

54

ACROSS

1 Storybook animal
6 Ollie's pal
10 Tennis great
14 Davy Jones's realm
15 Singer Patti
16 Payoff position at Belmont
17 Start of a quote from "Hamlet"
20 Rent
21 Work at steadily
22 One making a goal
23 Light-Horse Harry
24 They give deductions
26 Quote: Part II
30 Core
31 Like kitsch
32 Actual being
36 Beef order
37 Melodies
38 Quarters for Leo
39 Coffee servers
40 Skirt style
41 Corporeal channel
42 Quote: Part III
44 _____ Cup (yachting prize)
48 Road-sign abbr.
49 Spanish wine city
50 "Much _____ About Nothing"
51 Henry IV's birthplace
54 End of quote
58 Darling of the demos
59 Be pleased by
60 Unaccompanied
61 Poker pair
62 Antony's friend
63 Yarns

DOWN

1 Orange or Rose
2 Pain's partner
3 Track tournament
4 Outlaw
5 Scrutinize
6 Nimble
7 Sailor
8 Long, long _____
9 Predawn workers
10 Neckwear
11 Beach
12 "Iliad" author
13 Pitchers
18 Bread spread
19 "Off with you!"
23 Instruments playing false notes?
24 Phones again
25 Involve necessarily
26 Done, for short
27 Lend an ear
28 Merit
29 Boat basin
32 Emulate Juliet
33 Hindu garment
34 House location
35 Time periods
37 Showing good will
41 Elaine's town
42 Omen
43 "Das Rheingold" role
44 Limits
45 Bea Arthur role
46 Singer John
47 Tracks
50 Sweetsop
51 Louganis's milieu
52 Shakespeare's wife
53 Employs
55 Broadcast
56 Bout ending: Abbr.
57 Dockworkers' org.

55

ACROSS

1 Bagel
5 W.W. II servicewomen
9 Picket
13 "The _____ Love"
14 Where to seek what's chic
15 Approve
16 Warm-up for Winfield
19 Beings
20 Impish doings
21 Understands
22 Not _____ (zilch)
23 Assagais
26 Slipcover material
30 Thane's group
31 Eastern inn
32 Anguilliform creature
33 Swimming stroke
37 Montpellier Mrs.
38 Poet Dickinson
39 Nautical term
40 Hinged hooks
42 Wall boards
44 Horseshoe part
45 Is busy
46 Quite sore
49 Bayou craft
53 He aims high
55 "Stole _____ ..."
56 Cenobites
57 Tortosa's river
58 N.B.A. team
59 Becomes the plaintiff
60 T.V.A. works

DOWN

1 Bishop's wear
2 _____ even keel
3 Daugavpils native
4 Court principal
5 Reportable income
6 Most of Switzerland
7 Supportive
8 Garden legume
9 Vichyssoise base
10 Analogous
11 "Good counsellors _____ no clients": Shak.
12 Sizes up visually
14 Swivets' kin
17 Where Pompey rode
18 He's quick on the flaw
22 Marshal
23 Trickster
24 Egret's pride
25 Atelier prop
26 Provides an overhead
27 English hymnologist John Mason _____
28 Staircase feature
29 Les femmes
31 Move furtively
34 Eat one's words
35 Blends
36 Paid kidnappers
41 Wedding-cake features
42 Does some handwork
43 Both: Prefix
45 Yokels
46 To _____ (as one)
47 Handle harassment
48 Quatre et quatre
49 Boleyn or Hathaway
50 Mr. Eban
51 Semester
52 Hit signs
54 Gambler's marker

56

ACROSS

1 Joke
5 L.A. plague
9 Censor
12 Arm bone
13 Kind of boat or buoy
14 Prefix for stock or horn
16 Memorable name in fashion
17 Knowledge, for short
18 Thrust
19 Gape
20 Turn right
21 Peelers
22 Command re an option
25 Semihard, light yellow cheese
27 Mine product
28 Oriental nurses
29 Adages
31 German earth
35 Command re an option
38 Chemical suffixes
39 French ones
40 One who ties shoes
41 Stop on the RR
42 Civil
43 Command re an option
49 Incarnation
50 Bolivian export
51 Japanese aborigine
54 Full of grooves, as a road
55 Small lake
56 Adolescent
57 Certain Swiss paintings
58 Three wise men
59 Author Bagnold
60 Schedule abbr.
61 Dele's opposite
62 W.W. II town

DOWN

1 Punch's partner
2 Lamb
3 Raindrop's cousin
4 Discolors
5 Insult
6 Actor from N.Y.C.: 1939–76
7 Bid
8 Earthy prefix
9 Words on a book jacket
10 Asphyxia
11 Pola of silents
14 Winged
15 Aerie
21 Pocketbook
23 Mexican's enthusiastic affirmative
24 Monks' hoods
25 London gallery
26 "_____ Old Cowhand"
29 Radar's kin
30 Exist
31 Rates
32 Donee
33 Regimen
34 To be, in Lyon
36 Private instructor
37 "Thanks _____!"
41 Neuters
42 Critic
43 Urban oasis
44 Palate section
45 Spud
46 Speak
47 Ermine in summer
48 Fastener
52 Armstrong or Diamond
53 Ruin
55 Aft. periods

57

ACROSS

1 Wall Street term
6 Worker's recompense
10 Ball of yarn
14 The real "Funny Girl"
15 "_____ Old Cowhand"
16 Well-ventilated
17 Eliminated the squeaks
18 Between-meals snack
19 Ditto
20 Comedian Brooks
21 Nifty, to a flapper
24 Rich fabric
26 Kind of nose
27 Dishwasher's partner
28 Having talons
32 Dillon in "Gunsmoke"
34 "No, _____!"
37 Info at J.F.K.
38 Gives the green light
40 Actress Caldwell
41 Daft
43 Zilch
44 Smart and 99
47 Wharton School degs.
48 Turkish river
50 Of queenly bearing
52 Begin urban renewal
54 "What's _____?": Juliet
57 Union bosses' bunks?
61 For: Lat.
62 Bail
63 Take a tour: Abbr.
64 Fodder vessel, in Glasgow
66 Exploitative person
67 Prefix with phone or gram
68 Coeur d'_____, Idaho
69 Tot's counting word
70 German river
71 Steel-mill employee

DOWN

1 Enola Gay's cargo item
2 Judge
3 Day-Hudson comedy: 1959
4 Top pitcher
5 Terminal figure
6 Add chains, snow tires, etc.
7 Bible book
8 Struggles to speak
9 What makeup may do
10 Melon variety
11 Author O'Flaherty
12 Humorist Bombeck
13 Followers of exes
22 Picnic quaffs
23 Mint _____
25 Kind of slicker
29 He puts a damper on things
30 Kett of comics
31 When Dracula sleeps
32 A Lisa
33 Similar
35 Quarterback Jaworski
36 Golden _____
39 _____ Bernhardt
42 Muscat is its capital
45 Name for a newspaper
46 Transmit
49 Cross-city roadway
51 Hot-air artist
53 Committed a faux pas
55 Gosnold touched it in 1602
56 Mideast V.I.P.
57 Place to see Santa?
58 Alleviate
59 Yemeni seaport
60 Hay bundle
65 _____ bonne heure! (right!)

ACROSS

1 Snap up
5 Covent Garden offering
10 Sullen
14 Actress Keeler
15 Mulcts
16 Coin in Cremona
17 Baal, e.g.
18 A square, like Caspar Milquetoast
20 Contrive
22 Solemn
23 Snare
26 Golfer's cheapest purchase
27 Wordsworth's " . . . Tintern _____"
29 Kind of material
31 "Where there ____ no Ten Commandments": Kipling
35 Kin of Bronx cheers
36 Havoc
38 By way of
39 Eastern title
40 A square, à la Sinclair Lewis
41 "_____ Let Them Clash," Burns poem
42 Sun. text
43 Soporific
44 Suffix with ascend
45 Plane starter
47 Rickenbacker, for one
48 In a quandary
49 Yuk!
51 Rank below baronet
53 A splitting, as of atoms
57 Most recent
60 Foursquare
63 Assert
64 Pulitzer Prize author: 1958
65 Ostracize, in a way
66 Descartes
67 Kitten sounds
68 Avocet
69 Explosives

DOWN

1 Grating
2 Loutish
3 On the square
4 Reporters covet these
5 Tender
6 More, in music
7 Lineman
8 Autumn shades
9 Until now
10 More like stickum
11 Resort near Venice
12 Indic language
13 Baseball's Say Hey Kid
19 "I _____ that I dwelt . . .": Bunn
21 Farm enclosure
24 Lawrence of _____
25 Square up
27 Embarrass
28 Cinematic nickname
30 Blanch
32 All square
33 Sibling's daughter
34 Country singer Tucker
36 Chart
37 Nice summer
40 _____-woogie
44 Across
46 First prints of movies
48 Mellow
50 _____ up (hibernates)
52 Cove
53 Froth
54 "Bus Stop" creator
55 Fume
56 Ensuing
58 Dispatched
59 _____ bien
61 Seven, to Severus
62 Wright wing

59

ACROSS

1 Alpha follower
5 These may revolve
10 Canton is here
14 Let forth
15 Bandleader Shaw
16 Musical finale
17 Four score and five
19 Group of devotees
20 Bishops, e.g.
21 Breaks; rests
23 Ike's post in W.W. II
24 Cuba _____, rum drink
25 Frequently
27 Lowest pinochle card
30 Fearsome Greek goddesses
31 What 30 Across do
33 Beer's cousin
34 McEnroe vs. Connors
36 New Year's _____
37 _____ Mile Island
39 Biblical verb ending
40 Aid
43 Mighty mite
44 Tiny spores
46 Actor Calhoun and boxer Calhoun
48 Player-piano inserts
49 Ampersand
50 Hepplewhite product
52 Maeterlinck's "The _____"
57 R.I.P. notice
58 Dec. 31 figure
60 City in Alaska
61 Strong cord
62 Porter of Tin Pan Alley
63 Turned right
64 Drooping part of an iris
65 "If You _____ Susie . . ."

DOWN

1 Busy signal
2 Arabian bigwig
3 Buster Brown's dog
4 Part of N.C.A.A.
5 _____ Beach, Fla.
6 A fishbowl occupant
7 Elevator man
8 Miss. or Mo.
9 Action in osmosis
10 Happens
11 Common event on Dec. 31
12 Unemployed
13 Feed-bag filling
18 London art gallery
22 Red as _____
24 Wrinkles
25 Declaim
26 Cartoon figure on Dec. 31
27 Ben _____, Great Britain's highest peak
28 Bread spreads
29 Abound
30 Author Ben _____ Williams
32 Jerkins
35 Handel's birthplace
38 Book with a stiff cover
41 Chooses
42 Soprano from St. Louis
45 _____ swiss
47 Unique person
50 "Auld Lang Syne" is one
51 C. American tree
52 Radarscope signal
53 Chanteuse Horne
54 Take _____ the lam
55 Thespian's quest
56 Sketched
59 Flock member

60

ACROSS

1 Retirement accts.
5 Missile acronym
9 Mitigate
13 Hebrew bee
14 Asian capital
15 Checkup feature
16 Treaty org.
17 Preminger and Kruger
18 Garden "snake"
19 Avine collective
22 High, craggy hill
23 Propel a wherry
24 West Pointers
27 Command to a tailor
32 Yoga posture
33 Flag
34 Victorian or Edwardian
35 Feline collective
39 Summertime in N.Y.C.
40 November tally
41 Ignited anew
42 ". . . _____ and in his tongue": Shak.
45 Actress Ruth
46 Jimmy's successor
47 Emulate Howard
48 Ursine collective
55 Elevator man
56 _____ step, in dancing
57 Cloth measure
59 Marino-to-Duper play
60 Swinburne's "_____ the Microscope"
61 Den
62 Cafeteria need
63 Landlocked land
64 Poet Lazarus

DOWN

1 _____-Saud
2 Widen a hole
3 Aleutian island
4 _____ of the stick
5 Mother: Comb. form
6 Division word
7 This may be over your head
8 Memorable Italian director
9 Incite by argument
10 ". . . Indians, all in _____"
11 Lip
12 Give the once-over
14 Peasants, sometimes
20 Of a hope chest
21 Scandal sheet
24 Encrusted
25 Stage whisper
26 Alighieri
27 These raise Londoners
28 Berlin's Sommer
29 Soles' chasers
30 Banks on whom the Cubs banked
31 Weatherman's adjective
33 Presses a suit
36 Momentous
37 Armistice
38 Qualified to make a will
43 Ornate
44 Tellegen of silents
45 Nobelist in Chemistry: 1918
48 "Bright" inspiration for Keats
49 Actress Eilbacher
50 Tennis's Mandlikova
51 Word on a dollar bill
52 Z. Taylor and Tecumseh
53 Range
54 Pickings or Pickens preceder
55 Select
58 Between, in Bari

61

ACROSS

1 _____ Major
5 In excess
10 _____ mater
14 Get one's goat
15 Danger
16 Roulette bet at Monte Carlo
17 Expensive
18 Loathsome
20 Not important
22 Patterns
23 Soapstone
24 Assign by measure
25 Clean up
28 Decry
32 Metallic element
33 Italian province
35 Old horse
36 Old horses
38 Cheer in Cuernavaca
39 Low point
41 Goddess of dawn
42 Woolen fabric
45 Certain
46 Plausible
48 Writer Ortega y _____
50 Other
51 Evergreen
52 Queen Anne's lace, e.g.
55 Containers for lubricants
59 Strong aversion
61 Chamber-music ensemble
62 Comic-strip hero
63 Ordinary
64 Elbe feeder
65 Blackthorn
66 Untidy
67 Depression

DOWN

1 An Indic language
2 Nothing, in Nice
3 Eastern European
4 Making effervescent
5 Shoulder ornament
6 Mediterranean sailing ship
7 Trampled
8 Edge
9 Nourishment
10 Garland
11 Ear part
12 Factory
13 God of war
19 Brainstorm
21 Resinous substance
24 Sapper
25 Pan's appurtenances
26 Lowest deck
27 "To a _____," Burns poem
28 Greek island
29 A southern constellation
30 A neighbor of Sudan
31 Plumed heron
34 Picaroon
37 Mariner
40 Made a statement
43 Quack medicine
44 With legerity
47 Former Yankee
49 Computer gate
51 Type sizes
52 Broadway musical
53 Explorer Tasman
54 Flow: Comb. form
55 Burden
56 Exhort
57 Deportment
58 Separate carefully
60 Compass dir.

62

ACROSS

1 A high school, for short
5 Tartan design
10 W.W. I plane
14 Go on horseback
15 Frankie or Cleo
16 Rich material
17 Freeway spans
19 Jacob's twin
20 Fixes firmly
21 Lunch and dinner
23 Donkey, in Dijon
24 Building crossbeam
25 Stir up
30 Attaches
33 Diminutive
34 A soccer player
36 Strive
37 Rosary beads
38 Word with water or ground
39 Bona _____
40 Card spot
41 Villainous expression
42 Knight's helmet
43 Students, in St.-Lô
45 F.B.I. files
47 Prepares potatoes, in a way
49 Le jazz _____
50 Type of windlass
52 Chaffs
56 Hawaiian seaport
57 Track official
59 Part of a Jewish year
60 Roman magistrate
61 City near the Comstock Lode
62 Word with halcyon or salad
63 Exclude
64 Tennis segments

DOWN

1 Campus V.I.P.
2 _____ Ridge, 1972 Derby winner
3 W.W. II Greek resistance org.
4 Relates
5 Smoothed timber
6 Colleen
7 Some sloths
8 Sluggish
9 Renegade
10 Raveled silk
11 Spends, as an hour or day
12 One of a Latin trio
13 _____ ex machina
18 A bid for one's thoughts
22 Brace
25 Day's march
26 Author Shute
27 Bootleg by a quarterback
28 Ceil
29 Terminated
31 Mandate
32 Vetoes on the Volga
35 Stout's Mr. Wolfe
38 Deposed
39 Yankees' griddlecakes
41 Cult's cousin
42 Unisonally
44 Brims on caps
46 _____ Heights, Ohio
48 Slyly malicious
50 Libyan neighbor
51 Verdi masterpiece
52 Bartók or Lugosi
53 Fencing weapon
54 Torn
55 Hit-show signs
58 Playing marble

63

ACROSS

1 Apr. 15 collectors
4 Ottoman Empire founder
9 Kind of pipe
14 Detective Archer of fiction
15 Complete
16 Calm
17 Attend
18 Congreve comedy: 1695
20 Citrus coolers
22 Seiling of hockey
23 Midshipman
24 Savor
26 What sachets impart
27 Carpenter's friend
29 Hush!
30 Any bird
31 Kirghizian peaks
33 Ontario TV network
36 Ravel ballet: 1912
39 Heir pursuer
40 Entertainer Gillette
41 Forward
42 Electric-pen inv.
43 Siesta
44 Actress Gless
48 Misbehave
49 What a steed has
50 Trevino won this tournament in '84
51 Event at Hialeah
54 Consider seriously
57 Piper's son
58 Dancer Castle
59 Mrs. Kramden
60 N.T. Book
61 Relaxes
62 "The Screens" playwright
63 Alias, for short

DOWN

1 Ingrid's "Casablanca" role
2 Panpipe item
3 Jaye P. Morgan hit: 1956
4 Night person
5 Netman's apparel
6 "Kiss Me Quick" was one: 1969
7 Pianist Templeton
8 Ship-shaped clock
9 Cole Porter tune: 1929
10 "_____ Bayne," Foster song
11 High up
12 Tourist attractions near Carlsbad
13 Sidewalk superintendent
19 Source of vanilla
21 Conductor Caldwell
25 Koran supplement
26 _____ Na, musical group
27 Boggs of the Yankees
28 Gardner namesakes
29 It gets chalked
31 Pakistani, e.g.
32 Inadequate
33 Caesarion's mother
34 Ruth's husband
35 Relinquish
37 Altogether
38 Attack time
43 Like the nene
44 Frugal
45 Backpacks
46 "_____ We All?," 1929 song
47 Formal customs
48 "There, I've said It _____," 1941 song
49 Tumult
50 Mauna Loa goddess
52 Short-order man
53 Lady Hamilton
55 Termagant
56 Hanoi festival

64

ACROSS

1 Census fig.
5 Verb used with thou
10 Tiff
14 Showed up
15 Our place
16 Singing group
17 "_____ Three Lives": Philbrick
18 Brother, in Brest
19 Prefix with drome or dynamics
20 Cheese concoction
22 City in Denmark
24 Too unusual for words
27 Go to bed
28 Gaucho gear
31 _____ Vegas
34 Extinct bird
35 "The _____ Summer": Kahn
36 Expletive for Major Hoople
38 Designer Oscar de la _____
40 Alcohol additive
41 Prevents
43 Sea bird
45 Neither's partner
46 Chilean port
47 P.D.Q.
49 Looking backward
54 Kind of equation
55 African mammals, for short
56 Datum
57 Electron tube
60 Leave out
61 Gem shape
62 Table Bay is one
63 Store event
64 Depend
65 Curved moldings
66 Ogler

DOWN

1 Kind of film
2 Claw
3 Better
4 Famed British air marshal
5 Kin of apostates
6 Shell item
7 Prior, in poetry
8 Type of theatrical light
9 Bara of silents
10 British noble family
11 Like some exhibition games
12 River at Leeds
13 As well
21 Bought before
23 River into the Mediterranean
25 Sally of space trips
26 Laundry workers
29 Stir
30 At a distance
31 Wife of Tyndareus
32 Maturer
33 Like "Candide"
35 Small flags or important knights
37 In a proper manner
39 De _____ (superfluous)
42 _____ of exchange
44 Imprint
47 Pre-exam activity
48 Futile
50 Medium for "The Answer Man"
51 "Seven Days _____," 1964 film
52 Sheer fabric
53 Fragrant compound
54 Wash
56 "Tea _____ Two," Youmans song
58 Matador's encouragement
59 Actor Billy _____ Williams

65

ACROSS

1 Ancient Syria
5 La _____, opera house
10 Hyde or Central
14 Weighty work
15 Group of speakers
16 Woodwind with nasal tones
17 Had creditors
18 Relating to eight
19 Cinder
20 Start of a line by Tennyson
23 Quote
24 Pop
25 Chant
28 Lofty
33 Portuguese saint
34 Kelly or Moore
36 The clear sky
37 Food fish
39 More painful
41 Seine feeder
42 Calamities
44 Some subs
46 "Cara _____," 1954 song
47 Misleads
49 Poked quickly
51 "_____ Maria"
52 Toothed item
53 End of 20 Across
60 Cab
61 Des Moines native
62 Utilizer
63 Capital of South Yemen
64 Aromatic plant
65 Close
66 "Let freedom _____"
67 Disabled
68 _____ souci

DOWN

1 Minute particle
2 Up-front group of seats
3 So be it
4 Italian doctor
5 Shoplifters' nemeses
6 Hidden stores
7 Pot builder
8 Girl's name meaning "weary"
9 Refer (to) indirectly
10 Be subsequent to
11 Qualified
12 Leo's lament
13 Ten-gallon cask
21 "Of Thee I _____"
22 Hub of a wheel
25 Surrounded by water
26 Ingenuous
27 Gin and _____
28 Beiges
29 Onionlike herb
30 Little Tom
31 Spooky
32 Fear greatly
35 First-class
38 Coruscant
40 Answered
43 Hindu god
45 Certain U.S. weapons
48 Pardonable
50 Rifles' kid brothers
52 Thriller episode
53 Gully, usually dry
54 Conestoga team
55 New Rochelle college
56 Sink or _____
57 On the Coral
58 Shabby
59 Makes mistakes
60 Gob

ACROSS

1 St. Peter has one at St. Peter's
5 Domesticates
10 Ashen
14 Indigo
15 Endure
16 African river
17 Item in a corset or a collar
18 Oregon or Santa Fe
19 G.I.'s ration in W.W. II
20 Short wave?
21 Actress Anouk _____
22 Ornamental pattern, in art
23 An appetizer
26 Distillates of turpentine
29 Regimen
30 A.k.a.
31 Río de la _____
33 Form of communication?
36 An entree
39 Haw's partner
40 Aerial maneuvers
41 Kind of tube or sanctum
42 Stimulates, with "up"
43 Staid
44 A breakfast sweet
49 Homer's "Odyssey," e.g.
50 "_____ war": F.D.R.
51 Spar
55 Enjoy the warmth
56 Stendhal hero
57 Pizarro victim
58 Corner
59 Type of sodium carbonate
60 Glacial ridges
61 Rumpus
62 Mexican gentleman
63 Zola's courtesan

DOWN

1 Metal fastener
2 Stake
3 Ananias, e.g.
4 Greek god
5 A Turkic-speaking people
6 Shelters, in Savoie
7 City in Dade County
8 Widow of Ernie Kovacs
9 Variety of gypsum
10 Tailor's inserted piece
11 Drive off
12 Tex. shrine
13 Middle Eastern republic
24 Stores grain
25 More crumbly or powdery
26 Reckless
27 Ancient leather flask
28 Thailand, formerly
31 Morning star
32 Prune
33 Alcohol burner
34 Printer's mark
35 Marquette was one
37 Specious reasoners
38 Poem by Keats
42 Harvester of a kind
43 Like a stone pillar
44 I.O.U.'s
45 Separated
46 Japanese-American
47 Older brother of Moses
48 Mem. of a pool
52 Handle for Hadrian
53 Scrutinize
54 Scarlett's home

67

ACROSS

1 Royal Norse name
5 Plucky
9 Noggin
13 Betel palm
14 "A _____ Able"
15 _____ de la Société
16 _____ Major
17 Dispatched
18 Crooks' nemeses
19 Hayseed
21 Cypress feature
22 Wkly. arrival
23 "My Sister _____"
25 Rabbit fur

28 The first Mrs. Soames Forsyte
30 Crèche figures
31 Ablative, e.g.
33 Horatian creation
37 Slipped away
39 Washington's German baron
41 Poorest
42 Concerning
44 "Of Thee I _____"
45 Eight gills
47 Squander
49 Philatelists' books

52 Kiln
54 Liquori specialty
55 Killjoy
61 Iris part
62 Syllogism word
63 Broader
64 Submerge
65 Carol
66 Crème de la crème
67 Kin of Ph.D.'s
68 Russian agency
69 Quebec's Lévesque

DOWN

1 Buccal
2 Marquisette's weave
3 Citric _____
4 Queen Esther's predecessor
5 Quebec peninsula
6 Bacteria-free state
7 Mesabi hole
8 Veal Parmesan, perhaps
9 Crosspatch
10 Solitary
11 Caddoan abode
12 Ruhr center
13 C.P.A.'s record

20 Sixteen drams
24 Arrow poison
25 "Le Roi d'Ys" composer
26 Culture medium
27 Squirts
29 Symbol for André Watts
30 Garfield's sound
32 Shebat's follower
34 R.I.P. notice
35 Basso Jozsef _____
36 M.I.T. grad.
38 Anagram of must
40 Crying _____

43 Comical trio
46 Agreement
48 Retort
49 Titillate
50 Lead-colored
51 Mingle
53 Early stringed instruments
56 Malay outrigger
57 Heap
58 Frigg's mate
59 Network of nerves
60 Sei halved

68

ACROSS

1 Stout
4 Tiff
8 Thespian
13 Cutie
15 Sandarac
16 Not a soul
17 Five-and-ten
19 Sag
20 Heaven: Comb. form
21 Braun and Sydow
23 Mineral deposits
24 Tightwad
27 Story
28 Blood-hued
32 Neckpiece
35 Newport, R.I., has one
37 Daft
38 Tightly together
43 Water wheel
44 Compass pt.
45 Permit
46 "Fear God, and _____ commandments": Eccl. 12:13
49 Forum frock
52 Type of bread
57 Con game
60 African antelope
61 Saki
62 Pivotal
64 Social affair
66 Express a view
67 Some Feds
68 Being
69 Young adults
70 Assists
71 "Take _____, She's Mine"

DOWN

1 Total
2 France's longest river
3 Violinist Mischa
4 Posed
5 Sphere
6 Baseball's Hank
7 Ditch
8 Response to a ques.
9 Pigment
10 Travel
11 "Don't tread _____"
12 Agts.
14 Dustin Hoffman role
18 Salty sauce, British style
22 Haggard heroine
25 Paid athletes
26 Arabian prince
29 Asian weight
30 Concerning
31 "_____ la vie!"
32 Rowers' bench
33 Indian of Okla.
34 Farm measure
36 Mil. unit
39 U.S. journalist: 1889–1974
40 Waikiki's isle
41 Not discovered
42 Long period
47 Devilish tot
48 Ancient Laconian city
50 Furniture trimming
51 Kind of angle
53 Varnish base
54 Baked dough with filler
55 Jagged
56 Hermit
57 Blemish
58 Get by
59 "I cannot tell _____"
63 _____ judicata
65 U.S.N.A. graduate

69

ACROSS

1 Narrated
5 Sheepfolds
10 Squint
14 León's love
15 City near Kobe
16 Longfellow's bell town
17 Gnomish, in a way
18 Oscar winner: 1958
19 Havoc
20 Battologizes
22 Dorm topic
24 Beyond
25 Frat topic
26 Cudgels
29 British orderly
33 Azimuth
34 Strikebreaker
36 Cinched
37 Snail's motto
41 Bristles
42 Parrot
43 Diminutive suffix
44 Imply
46 Gone, at Logan
49 Tommy of the theater
50 Deliver a haymaker
51 Gust
54 Game fish
58 Be bested
59 "... _____ face the world with": Browning
61 Gallimaufry
62 Actuaries' concerns
63 Silk voile
64 Rod's partner
65 Siliques
66 Anthony and Clarissa
67 Nixed item

DOWN

1 Actor Jacques _____
2 Skip
3 Like an eremite
4 Decay in a forest
5 Italian noblewoman
6 Wicker
7 Hebrew letters
8 Duke Ellington's monogram
9 Huarache
10 Fa la, e.g.
11 Case for trivia
12 Banshee's bailiwick
13 "Lair" of two Baers
21 Harriman nickname
23 Let
25 Butler in 1939
26 Chaliapin and Moscona
27 "Over the Rainbow" composer
28 Apollo 15 astronaut
29 Scenic peninsula
30 Devout
31 St.-Cyr-l'_____
32 Fortification
35 Shipper's need
38 Carte carrier
39 Longest human bone
40 Ciceronian collection
45 "_____ for tennis?"
47 Kennel adjunct
48 Hereditary
50 Squelched
51 Tab
52 Trademark
53 Canceled, as a stamp
54 Tenor Maison
55 Dairyman's anathema
56 Vienna, to a Viennese
57 "Star Wars" hero
60 _____-nod (show drowsiness)

70

ACROSS

1 Solo
6 As well
10 Enjoy a quid
14 Distributed
15 Perches
16 Pedro's "Ahoy!"
17 "Festina lente"
20 Here, in Paris
21 Watery fluids
22 Zones
23 Eliot work
27 Director Howard

28 Squatter
32 Dali's homeland
35 Bank transaction
38 Site of the Tell legend
39 Saw
43 Berenson's subject
44 Pot item
45 Obliterate
46 Sly
49 Theater sign
50 Cornmeal mush
57 What a bigwig carries

60 Part
61 Nothing
62 Saw
66 Make eyes at
67 Brainstorm
68 Violinist Isaac
69 Brassie, e.g.
70 Cabbage; bread
71 He wrote "Too Late
   the Phalarope"

DOWN

1 Come clean
2 Cause filtering
3 Jack of old films
4 Mets' div.
5 Afr. country
6 Pecuniary resource
7 British measure
8 Swipe
9 W.W. II govt. agency
10 Combinations of tones
11 Inventor Elias
12 Singer Fitzgerald
13 What E. B. Browning
   counted
18 Org.
19 "Daily Planet"
   employee

24 Formal order
25 Tops
26 O'Neill's "_____
   Christie"
29 Popular sandwich
   filler
30 Aphrodite's son
31 Liturgy
32 Hit a gnat
33 Young salmon
34 Italian wine city
35 Chaney
36 Teammate of Bill
   Terry
37 Veneration
40 Negatives
41 A jerk

42 Trampled
47 Conveyed on a flume
48 Petruchio's wife
49 Takes to court
51 Commerce
52 Hayseed
53 Skirt part
54 Atlas feature
55 Explosive, for short
56 First orbiting American
57 Vittles
58 Como, to Carlos or
   Carlo
59 Frogner Park's locale
63 Soviet plane
64 O. Henry's monogram
65 One _____ time

71

ACROSS

1 Pitch indicator
5 Daughter of William the Conqueror
10 London's Albert _____
14 Emulate the good doctor
15 Gardener in spring
16 Nichols hero
17 With 57 Across, mason's lament
20 Recreation centers
21 Queen Gertrude's son
22 Grant obtained by Hollywood
23 In person
24 Leyte neighbor
27 Steeplejacks, at times
31 Antarctic cape
32 Gay deceiver
33 Australian honey possum
34 Small ape
35 Billet-doux opener
38 Norris Dam org.
39 Amazon dolphin genus
41 Something bankers lean on
42 Arabian prince
44 Mason's material
46 Jerks
47 Ambassadorial asset
48 Holier-_____-thou
50 Quit
53 When the lunch bunch munch
57 See 17 across
59 Sorrel's kin
60 Shopper's concern
61 Leave Logan
62 Sounds of disapproval
63 Snake genus
64 Laurel bestowed on Hollywood

DOWN

1 Modish
2 Woman in a Yeats poem
3 Make one's salt
4 A caboose preceder
5 Role for Walters
6 Soft and fluffy
7 Mas that say "maa"
8 Wimbledon call
9 D.C. building
10 Sam Spade's creator
11 Former labor leader
12 Verse
13 A Balt
18 Came closer
19 Chalet feature
23 Compare
24 Franks' _____ law
25 "A Bell for _____"
26 S.F. Bay county
27 Street show
28 Horner or Sprat
29 Split
30 Top bananas
32 "Pajama Game" actor
36 Optional course
37 Lessee
40 They outshout words
43 Coaches
45 Harum-scarum
48 Do some sums
49 Fire-engine gear
50 Tapered tuck
51 Biblical oldster
52 Neb. neighbor
53 V. Lopez theme song
54 Monogram pt.
55 Cartouche
56 Place west of Nod
58 N.T. book

148

72

ACROSS

1 Rival of Ole Miss
5 After, in Arles
10 Ghanaian seaport
14 Ancient kingdom
15 Literary Becky
16 First governor of "The 49th"
17 French magazine
18 Short-legged dog
19 Presswork with pix
20 Strain
22 Jayhawker
24 Pueblo Indian
25 Joyous celebration
26 Yields as a return
28 Birthstone
33 Grasped
35 Item often having interest
36 Sine _____
37 Formerly, once
38 Homophone for a biblical queen
40 Body
41 "Pink Marsh" author
42 Conductor Klemperer
43 Blackjack player's opponent
45 Birthstone
48 Chevet
49 Am. call-up outfit
50 File
52 Crow's kin
55 Tempestuous winds
59 Vent
60 Craft
62 Brainstorm
63 Anagram of noel
64 Corroded
65 Wagnerian cycle
66 _____ out (barely managed)
67 "_____ thou these great buildings?": Mark 13:2
68 Major ending

DOWN

1 Gripe
2 "I am monarch of _____ survey"
3 Promenade
4 Birthstone
5 B.M.I. rival
6 Caused by light
7 Choice
8 Unit of work
9 Plant of the ginseng family
10 Core
11 Selves
12 So long, in Soho
13 Shortly
21 "Second Hand _____"
23 Solar disk
25 Cleaving tool
26 Lost to view
27 Goose genus
29 Choral singers
30 Fans' favorites
31 Evangelist McPherson
32 Stingy
33 In the catbird _____
34 Explodes
39 Slammer
40 Birthstone
42 Expel
44 Maugham's "_____ of Suez"
46 Named a price
47 Gullies
51 Common contraction
52 Take out
53 Berserk
54 Cattle, to Cowper
55 N.B.A.'s Archibald
56 Emulate Edward Bok
57 Cleft
58 Kind of brush
61 Charlotte from Milwaukee

73

ACROSS

1 Venue
5 "Cave _____"
10 Radar signal
14 Genus of freshwater fish
15 Three-time A.L. batting champ
16 Punjabi potentate
17 Border on
18 Talent for making millions
20 Ornamental handwork
22 All-day rains
23 Belle taken to Troy
24 As to
25 Cotton cloth
27 Called on
31 Eating area
32 Keynes's topic
33 Browning's "_____ Bratts"
34 Fiddler-crab genus
35 Become greater
40 Tidied (up)
44 Famed twister of words
45 Throws out
46 Dante illustrator
47 What the toxophilite did
48 Characteristic marks
51 Burst inward
54 Criterion
56 Pitcher
57 Two-toed sloth
58 Passover feast
59 Cozy
60 Jupati, e.g.
61 Hebrew months
62 Tupolevs, for short

DOWN

1 Part of a baseball
2 Russian hut
3 Iffy
4 Ultra
5 Remark
6 Property-title receiver
7 Nest, in Nice
8 Not straightforward
9 Of a secret society
10 Trained; oriented
11 Nobelist in Physics: 1914
12 Addition: Abbr.
13 Cries of contempt
19 Ankle: Comb. form
21 Got out of the saddle
25 Ferber et al.
26 Mooring place
28 Scores of autumnal scores
29 Role at a roast
30 Pairs
36 Bit
37 Philanthropist Pratt
38 Gratiano's bride
39 Handled
40 Hue man
41 Elementary texts
42 Sloping walkway
43 Nugatory
48 "Rip _____," Presley hit
49 Singer-songwriter Hendryx
50 Like certain controls
52 O.T. book
53 Energy units
55 Scheherazade slept here

74

ACROSS

1 Mexican food
6 Exotic bird
10 Injure
14 Harden
15 Manganese and malachite
16 Curved molding
17 Meditated, with "over"
18 "Pop ____ the weasel"
19 Facts
20 Mixture
22 Deg. holder
23 Weight in India
24 Hammer
26 Kitchen gadget
30 Organize
32 Dog that went to Oz
33 Notices
35 Nocturnal lemur
39 Displayed
41 Matriculator
43 Islamic spiritual center
44 Impression
46 Golden ____ of the West Coast
47 Sequence
49 Trample
51 Force
54 Princely Italian house
56 Sanction
57 Mixture
63 Roast: Fr.
64 Gaelic
65 Nigerian seaport
66 Def. alliance
67 So be it
68 Quibble
69 School on the Thames
70 Ointment-yielding plant
71 Not so common

DOWN

1 Apexes
2 Puzzler's favorite ox
3 Ringlet
4 Utah city
5 Collected
6 V.I.P.
7 Historical period
8 Penury
9 Help
10 Mixture
11 Henry ____ Wallace
12 Place a new label on
13 Victor at Gettysburg
21 Prickly evergreen shrub
25 A knockout
26 Goblet part
27 World spinner
28 Suffix with Ham or Shem
29 Mixture
31 Sum ____ fui . . .
34 One of the Adamses
36 Harvest
37 "____ each life . . ."
38 British gun
40 Reiner or Sagan
42 Morsel
45 Backstage employee
48 Lower in dignity
50 Bank employee
51 Seine tributary
52 Untersee craft
53 Argument
55 Lurch forward on heavy seas
58 "My Friend ____"
59 Mount St. Helens production
60 Thickening agent
61 Protuberance
62 Belgian canal connector

75

ACROSS

1 Down Under birds
5 Jai-alai basket
10 Down Under product
14 A Carnegie
15 "Wait _____ Dark"
16 Pelvic bones
17 "The _____" (subject of this puzzle)
20 Even if, for short
21 Modify to suit
22 Requires
23 Preminger product
24 High _____ kite
25 Koala's "kitchen"
33 Indigo dyes
34 Consumer
35 Numbat's morsel
36 Brief autobiography
37 Drafty places
39 "Money _____ object"
40 When Paris sizzles
41 Stopper
42 Ancient Greek theater
43 1988 bicentennial city
47 Unmatched
48 Amateur radio operators
49 Diving apparatus
52 "And the rockets' red _____ . . ."
54 Half a dance
57 Southern lights
60 Alum
61 Prospect
62 Suva is its capital
63 Supporter
64 Allen or Frome
65 Down Under marsupials

DOWN

1 Prepare for publication
2 Long-run TV show
3 Indians' shell money
4 Tasman or Timor
5 Lovable
6 Bivouac
7 Traffic sign
8 Hue
9 Hgt.
10 One-dimensional
11 To the sheltered side
12 Obey
13 Cricket equipment
18 Fastens
19 Tchr.
23 F.D.R. dog
24 "_____ Death": Grieg
25 Lower borders of roofs
26 Oneness
27 Quoted
28 Finnish port
29 Seagoing org.
30 Supporting frame
31 Boredom
32 Mouthlike opening
37 He played Hopalong
38 Brazilian macaw
39 One of the Argonauts
41 Fragrant wood
42 Abalone
44 Not a soul
45 Kind of daisy
46 Scottish garment
49 Tale of derring-do
50 Ringlet
51 Russian river
52 Rate; speed
53 Luxuriant
54 Muse of history
55 Son, in Buenos Aires
56 Sale sign
58 St.
59 Neighbor of Eur.

156

76

ACROSS

1 Boiler product
6 "The _____," play by Aristophanes
11 Commando
13 Moves stealthily
15 Hairy
16 Eightfold
17 Freer display at D.C.
18 Comments
20 A source of rubber
21 Tailless amphibian
23 Certain palms
24 Luge
25 Cahn output
27 Atl. City marker
28 Hon
29 Seamstress's utensil
32 Former republic of NE Africa
33 They, in Paris
34 Useless but costly object
41 Gleamed
42 Actor Chaney
43 Work translated by Pope
45 Sagacious
46 Chart again
48 In _____ (wholly)
49 Triple this for a wine
50 Cuddly
52 Heat unit, for short
53 Abstract
55 British motor trucks
57 Figure on Louisiana's seal
58 Gourmet's cousin
59 Amber is one
60 Coal beds

DOWN

1 Saddle appendage
2 Richly embellished ice cream
3 Sounds of hesitation
4 River between Manchuria and Russia
5 Allots
6 Candle fibers
7 Some are co-ops
8 Alphabetic trio
9 Demotic
10 Late British movie star
11 Part of an arrow
12 Stay
13 Muscular
14 Unkempt
19 Highly excited
22 Authentic
24 Seasoning obtained by evaportation
26 Ray
28 Territory in N India
30 Spleen
31 Roof angle
34 Susurrus
35 Antagonistic
36 Ace, as part of a blackjack
37 Hill in the Southwest
38 Make possible
39 Element used in alloy steels
40 Shreds
41 Long oar
44 Drench
46 Kind of numeral
47 Drops heavily
50 Sites: Abbr.
51 O'Neill's _____ Smith
54 Las' followers
56 Bldg. in Rockefeller Center

77

ACROSS

1 Cinches
6 Rainwater pipe
11 Almost a knight: Abbr.
14 Soda pop in Boston
15 One of the Keys
16 Trifle
17 De Sica's "Yesterday, Today _____"
19 Celestial dessert?
20 Actor Turhan _____
21 Domino or Waller
22 "_____ Well . . ."
23 Proust's "Remembrance _____"
27 Scrutinizes
30 Like some cookies
31 Cupid
32 Indian city
33 "Honest" one
36 Beckett classic
41 Draft letters
42 Young horse
43 Bartók or Lugosi
44 Kind of inflection
46 Halts
49 Dylan's "_____ Are A-Changin'"
52 Achilles or Ajax
53 Take _____ the lam
54 Goal
57 Outer: Comb. form
58 Dali's "_____ of Memory"
62 Fire: Fr.
63 Basilica area
64 A de Mille
65 Football pts.
66 Cotton thread
67 Good earth

DOWN

1 Pierce
2 "And Then There Were _____"
3 Warhol or Williams
4 Pendulum's partner
5 Flouts
6 Lazy arboreal clingers
7 Iranian dialect
8 Hockey great
9 Actor Tognazzi
10 Haul
11 Shore-front walkways
12 Stains
13 Pursuit
18 The end, in chess
22 Copy
23 Eject
24 NASA's "not ready"
25 Teri of "Tootsie"
26 Kind of party
27 Seats for the faithful
28 Guidry stats.
29 Carousing noisily
32 C.I.O.'s partner
34 Nut's complement
35 Airport abbrs.
37 Province ceded to Morocco
38 Linguist Chomsky
39 Strong wind
40 "_____ thy heart": Emerson
45 Ear: Comb. form
46 Raiment
47 Pi-sigma connectors
48 Kind of library
49 "Property is _____!": Proudhon
50 Jinxed
51 Rope fiber
54 Henry VIII's second
55 Some desserts
56 Gob's meal
58 Chum
59 Yalie
60 Wall St. abbr.
61 Kind of trip

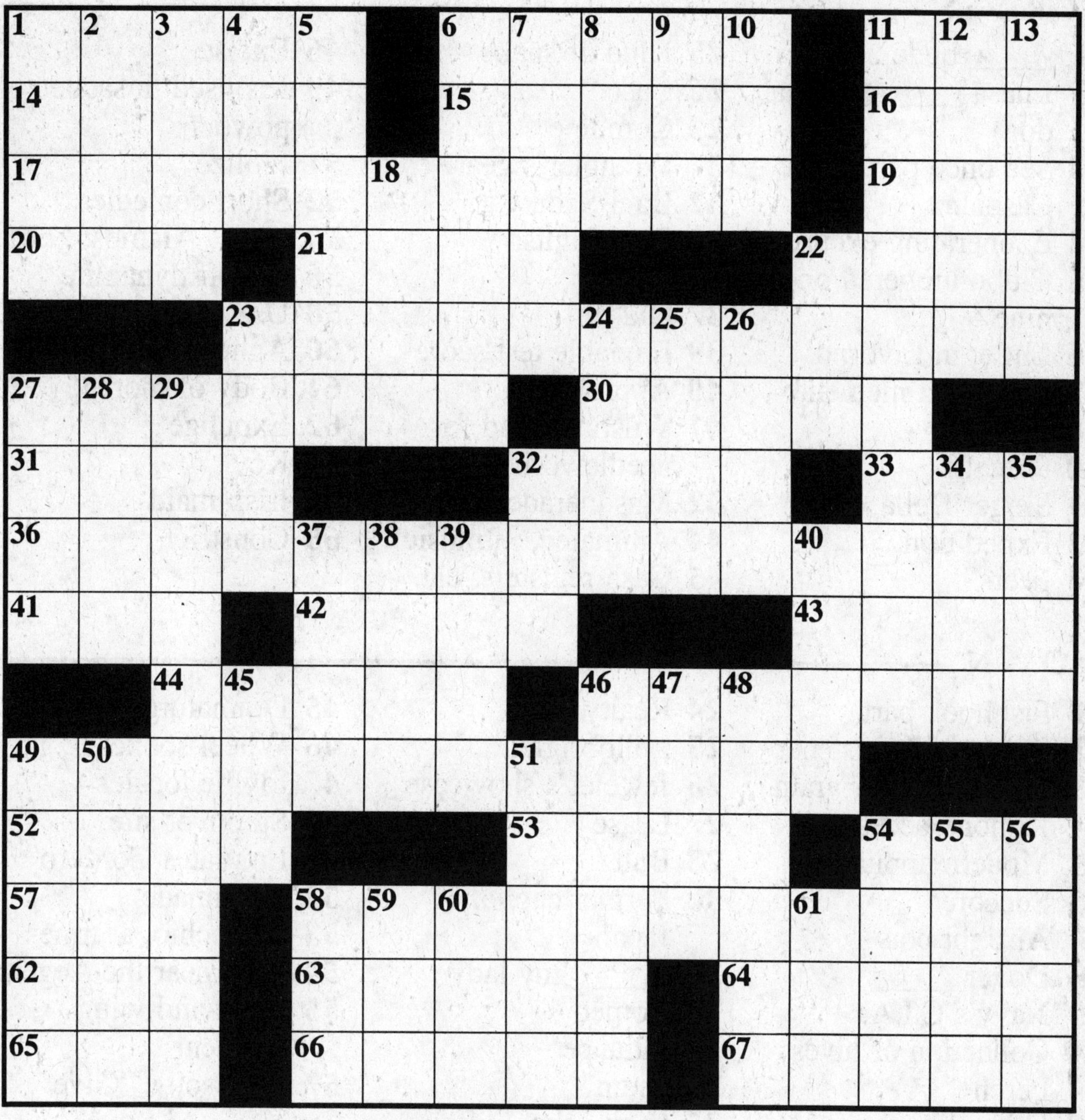

78

ACROSS

1 _____ buddies
6 Lhasa _____ (Tibetan dog)
10 Sea once part of the Caspian
14 Exonerating excuse
15 Club numbered one to nine
16 Little, in Livorno
17 Treasured memento
18 Tasty
20 Catcall
21 Singer Della
23 Expedition
24 Peers
25 Kind of snake
26 Cast
29 Combine
31 Wrangler's gear
32 Bani-Sadr, e.g.
33 Speed inits.
36 Equip
37 Old pro
39 Enviable test score
40 Approval
41 Wilson famed for needlework
42 Masquerade ensemble
44 Animated, in music
45 Cash registers, e.g.
46 Excise
49 Iris used in sachet powder
51 Idolize
52 Short comedies
53 _____ Alamos, N.M.
56 Set off dynamite
58 Use a block and tackle
60 Agnes, in Acapulco
61 Body of mores
62 Expunge
63 Key
64 Irish maid
65 Constrict

DOWN

1 Fishhook part
2 Sandwich moistener
3 Storehouse for grain
4 Kimono accessory
5 Modern appliance
6 Succored
7 Airtight pots
8 Dover _____
9 Navy's C.I.A.
10 Collection of hives
11 Perch
12 Critical
13 Ne'er-do-well
19 Food warmers
22 Sea accipiter
24 Realty unit
25 Lollobrigida
26 Jeweler's showcase
27 Lease
28 Butts
30 Former capital of Japan
32 "_____ my lady . . .": Romeo
33 Pittance
34 Teem
35 High-school affairs
38 Celtic language
43 Begley and Asner
44 Glum
45 Dramaturgy, for one
46 Wheel spokes, e.g.
47 Idyllic locales
48 Stopover site
50 Emulates Cordero
52 Colonnade
53 Pinocchio, at times
54 Peak near the Aegean
55 Buck-and-wing segment
57 Emerson's "Give _____ to Love"
59 Smidgen for Spot

79

ACROSS

1 Dummies
5 Legal offenses
9 Fleece
14 Viva voce
15 Suffix for axiom
16 Bandleader James
17 Ind. city
18 Ex–Strawberry patch?
19 Incensed
20 Manacles manipulator
23 Tennyson product
24 Abstract being
25 Airport label for Caracas
28 Essen exclamation
31 Fodder for Freud
33 Paducah's river
34 Macbeth title
36 New York inst.
37 Wood: Comb. form
38 Politician, publisher and P.M.
42 Heroic poetry
43 Corrode
44 Framework
45 Colorful river
46 December sight
49 Part of i.e.
50 To boot
51 Pop's partner
52 Author Rand et al.
54 Screenwriter for "Accident": 1967
59 European heath
62 Lover's sound
63 Without, in Dresden
64 Corporate checkup
65 Gen. Robert _____
66 Foray
67 Malamud product
68 Pool in a range
69 Completes

DOWN

1 One of the recent frosh
2 Kind of code
3 Henry VIII's last wife
4 Drink noisily
5 Kitchen utensil
6 Reception
7 Place
8 Brahms's "_____ Festival"
9 Climbs, in a way
10 Spydom's Zelle
11 Failed amendment
12 Cinematics, e.g.
13 Caulfield's spot
21 Vaud vibrato
22 Briefly
25 With 30 down, Byronic pilgrim
26 Cheroots
27 Petrarch specialty
28 Adviser to Odysseus
29 "Motherhood" painter
30 See 25 Down
32 Having wings
33 Stewpot
35 Kind of cone or dive
39 Inigo Jones concern
40 Long-tailed monkey
41 Tribe conquered by the Romans
47 Sponge
48 Well-known mark
51 Chayefsky's butcher
53 Zzzzz
54 Prince Charles is one
55 Actress Kedrova
56 Larger _____ life
57 Author Bagnold
58 Beatty movie
59 _____-relief
60 Boring routine
61 Half a musical title

80

ACROSS

1 Stock trader's aid
6 The younger Guthrie
10 Three-handed card game
14 Western flick
15 Kramer's "High _____"
16 Queen of Carthage
17 Gladiator's milieu
18 Valid
19 State of agitation
20 "Merry Oldsmobile" garb
23 Turn right
24 Players
25 Site of the appendix
27 What the Earps were
31 Flaherty's Nanook, for one
33 Celebes ox
34 Raced
36 Bout
39 Scornful one
41 Forewarned
43 Divide equally
44 Easter flower
46 Klondike lure
47 Pertaining to a holy season
49 Bordoni and Papas
51 Polk's successor
53 Frank Herbert novel
55 Boston, for O. W. Holmes
56 Jockey's work clothes
62 Crude metals
64 African republic
65 Brainstorms
66 Birthplace of Chang and Eng
67 "_____ kleine Nachtmusik": Mozart
68 Sparkle
69 Light brown
70 W.W. II servicewoman
71 Snug abodes

DOWN

1 Newcastle surfeit
2 Dutch-born spy
3 Egyptian sun god's symbol
4 M. Descartes
5 Medium's state
6 Cattle breed
7 Oscar role for Wayne
8 Rifle
9 Next at bat
10 Former campus activist org.
11 Mythical Dixie ruler
12 This fits with "Bon voyage!"
13 Clan symbol
21 Whom Beatrice guided through Paradise
22 Pay boost
26 Come forth
27 Cat
28 Actress Magnani
29 "Creepy" winter-weather forecaster
30 Comic-book captain
32 Circus performer
35 Heraldic band
37 Prefix meaning "distant"
38 Tote-board information
40 McCormack or Melchior
42 Situated
45 One of the Jones boys
48 Radar signals
50 Surrender at chess
51 "_____ were the days"
52 Like gold
54 Subordinate to
57 Approach shot at Doral
58 Kind of chatter
59 Hilo neckwear
60 German philosopher
61 Controversial planes
63 T.C.U. football rival

81

ACROSS

1 Cleveland or Lincoln
5 François's feather
10 Israeli seaport
14 Tony's cousin
15 Perlman purchase
16 Wind sound
17 Ustinov play
20 Greek nickname
21 He wrote "Metamorphoses"
22 Within, to Titus
23 Some Cowboys
25 Kind of fly
27 Wife of Aegir
28 Soupçon
29 Spiritual advisers
31 A case for Cicero: Abbr.
32 O.T. book
34 Luau dip
35 Let go
36 Vehicle for Swoosie Kurtz
39 Powder base
41 Highlander's own
42 Gelada or pongo
43 Ending for glamour or vapour
44 Vision
46 Potpourri ingredient
50 The youngest Cratchit
51 "_____ a Wonderful Life"
52 Resemble purposely
54 Parsley's kin
56 Greek letters
57 Banking acronym
58 They're open at some opens
62 Swenson of "Benson"
63 Father, to Virgil
64 Leg coverings
65 Irish tax
66 Of the same opinion
67 Leftovers for Lassie

DOWN

1 Metallic element
2 Spain and Portugal
3 Connections
4 Still
5 Put to the test
6 Book by Henry Green
7 No longer new
8 Mrs. Gump
9 Printers' measures
10 Word of assent
11 Like a certain Mary
12 Pessimist's struggle
13 Increase
18 ". . . and the _____ the brave?"
19 Waiter's take
24 System of principles
25 College V.I.P.
26 Séance board
30 "Once _____ Mattress"
33 Spring up
35 Fast
36 Peggy and Ian
37 Gets a wiggle on
38 Haughty
39 Enormous
40 Stupid
44 Worms, to an early bird
45 Potholder of a kind
47 He keeps one in stitches
48 Napping
49 Rents
53 Skiing family name
55 "I must down to the _____ again": Masefield
56 Inner: Comb. form
59 Conservation org.
60 Have a bite
61 Cry of discovery

82

ACROSS

1 Brouhaha
6 Bearded bloom
10 Head of France
14 Bird's abnormal wing
15 "Pygmalion" actor
16 Came to earth
17 High-class status symbol
19 "Twittering Machine" painter
20 Beauty's preceder
21 Atomic number 50
22 Shows up
24 Wreck completely

26 Betty followed her
27 Sardou play
30 Business costs
35 Vicinities
36 Pad of the pride
37 Within: Comb. form
38 Mil. officers
39 Parlor pieces
40 On _____ (available for duty)
41 Do a diaskeuast's job
42 Turgenev's birthplace
43 Badgerlike creature
44 Semi driver

46 Four-flushers
47 Wood for skis
48 Range
50 _____ peanuts
54 Be a tattletale
55 High note
58 Issue forth
59 Street urchin
62 Bona _____
63 Neighbor of Minn.
64 Chanticleer's realm
65 _____ boarder
66 About
67 Otherworldly

DOWN

1 A Roosevelt
2 Country dance
3 Regulation
4 Ultimate effort
5 Clerical figures
6 One of the Masseys
7 _____ López of chess fame
8 Manco Capac, for one
9 High-_____ (spirited horses)
10 Excel
11 First name in scat
12 Shea component
13 Summers on the Seine

18 "Educating _____," 1983 film
23 Palmer's concern
24 Dinner V.I.P.
25 Timberwolves
27 Gem side
28 Wear down
29 Author Ephron
31 Small glass container
32 Growing out
33 He established the Ethical Culture Society
34 Items from a cabbage patch?
36 Traditional knowledge

39 Actress Ann and family
43 Sheer ecstasy
45 Kennedy visitor
46 Firefighting substance
49 Short-billed bird
50 Rose Bowl "zebras"
51 Neglect
52 "O patria mia" source
53 Wall base
55 An _____ effort
56 Virna of films
57 Kitty's birth?
60 Whale group
61 Grant, to Lee

83

ACROSS

1 Obi
5 Muffles
10 Pahoehoe
14 Toast covering
15 Like argon
16 Desiccated
17 Mosel tributary
18 This may be posted
19 Violet container
20 Rosalind's lover
22 Prospero's servant
24 Little corn grower
25 Tree or resort
26 Pierre and Helena
30 Ruffs' cousins
34 Woody's son
35 Jeune fille
37 Intimidate
38 Spanish estuary
39 Concurs
41 Map abbr.
42 Transcript
44 Ombu or poon
45 Proper
46 Versants
48 Dandie Dinmonts
50 Acclaims
52 Baltique, e.g.
53 Desdemona's husband
56 Posthumus's servant
60 Hat-trick component
61 Prevent
63 Tide type
64 Jennifer of WKRP
65 Legendary being
66 Former Genovese magistrate
67 Joy's lioness
68 Utopias
69 Soon

DOWN

1 Just fair
2 Winged
3 Close securely
4 Hamlet's friend
5 Distribution problems
6 P. Wylie's "Night _____ Night"
7 Cachar, e.g.
8 Ambler and Knight
9 Renders penniless
10 "Titus Andronicus" heroine
11 Bedouin
12 Passport stamp
13 Yemeni capital
21 Common negative
23 Gives temporarily
25 Avers
26 Two-wheeled vehicles
27 Prospero's aide
28 Flat: Comb. form
29 Least likely
31 Vichyssoise, e.g.
32 Journalize
33 Instructions to a printer
36 Dirk of yore
39 Of a region
40 They can bring the house down
43 Polonius's daughter
45 Prospero's daughter
47 Some fodder
49 Dos' followers
51 "I _____ a lass . . .": Wither
53 Leer's kin
54 Dibble or burin
55 Painter Holbein
56 Sch. authority
57 Sign gas
58 Desdemona's detractor
59 Type of tournament
62 Dir. from Madrid to Barcelona

84

ACROSS

1 Hazard at sea
5 Comprehensiveness
10 Noah's first son
14 Summit
15 Kind of bear
16 German's great hall
17 "Till _____," 1946 film
20 Garden tool
21 City of SE France
22 Low-lying tracts
23 _____ vide (which see)
24 Houston or Snead
25 "Of _____ and starry skies": Byron
33 Refuge on a desert
34 Meadows
35 "_____ Yankee Doodle Dandy"
36 Nipa palm
37 Short trip
39 Chinese weight
40 Ord. to pay money
41 Buffs
42 Call
43 Have one's _____ (daydream)
47 River of Devon
48 Truth twister
49 Fiber for nets
52 Tribunal
54 Spirit of St. Louis
57 Weather forecast
60 City; town
61 Russian co-op
62 Wags
63 Allot
64 Elklike mammal
65 Visibility reducer

DOWN

1 High-school subj.
2 Chinese tree
3 Pintail duck
4 Gumshoe
5 Relating to certain seeds
6 Grand _____ Dam
7 Word with shoppe
8 Football tactic
9 Stray
10 Deli item
11 Pea pod
12 Magdeburg's river
13 Hall of Famer Willie _____
18 Praises
19 Stadiums, often
23 Cavil
24 Shoo!
25 Football's Noll or Knox
26 Shaping machine
27 Japan's greatest port
28 Melting snow
29 E.M.K. is one
30 Tabby's plaint
31 Correct
32 Certain transactions
37 Austen or Eyre
38 Formicid
39 Norse god of thunder
41 Repaired
42 "Republic" author
44 Big flood
45 Escapes
46 Ring
49 Mod. weapon
50 Veer; twist
51 Civil wrong
52 "_____ nome," Verdi aria
53 Not fooled by
54 Inter _____ (among other things)
55 City of NE France
56 Scotch Gaelic
58 Sweet potato
59 Monogram of the Great Dissenter

85

ACROSS

1 Chronicler of the Round Table
7 W.W. II lass
10 Poet Whitman
14 Site of Hejaz and Nejd
15 Cigar residue
16 The shivers
17 Captured again
18 Pirate immortal
20 Proofer's mark
21 Menotti opus: 1950
22 Ursa, to Juan
23 Go astray
25 Fifth spot in some theaters
26 "Roots" co-star
29 Gilmore of the N.B.A.
33 Vitriolic
35 Paradise for King Arthur
38 A Gardner
39 Pahlavi's title
40 Capitol toppers
41 Biting insect
42 Caboodle's partner
43 School discipline
44 Last of the Stuarts
45 Word with case or well
47 Dashing
49 Actress Patricia
52 Badger
53 Wheat beard
56 Britten's foretopman
60 Kind of surgeon
62 Union
63 Bane of an off-key tenor
64 Daniels of old films
65 One, in Köln
66 Countersign, e.g.
67 Bearish initials
68 Gleam
69 Paucity

DOWN

1 Polo
2 Districts
3 Verdi's fallen woman
4 Clarinet's relative
5 Disturber of the peace
6 Far East beast
7 Launder
8 Autumn bloomer
9 Extensive S.A. plain
10 Creator of 30 Down
11 Epochs
12 Alban Berg's femme fatale
13 Rossini's "William ____"
19 Dan of "Laugh-In"
21 Actress Claire
24 Author of "Hard Cash"
27 Anglo-Saxon letter
28 Belgian city
30 Visitor at Venusberg
31 Lendl of tennis
32 Assuage completely
33 Seeks to find out
34 Voucher
36 Capitalist-politician Stanford
37 Honshu port
41 Freon, e.g.
43 Norseman's Venus
46 A mass of stratified rock
48 Set afire
50 Doubleday or Dean
51 Sutherland role
54 Take by force
55 Sheree from L.A.
56 Hindu gentleman
57 Seine sights
58 Degrees for A.B.A. members
59 Gainsay
61 C' ____-dire
63 Possessed

86

ACROSS

1 "Gypsy Love" composer
6 Actress June
11 Fashionable resort
14 Omit
15 Dress designer Head
16 Judah Ben-_____
17 Principle of Martin
Luther
King Jr.
19 Cultural period
20 Composer Vivaldi
21 Actress Burstyn
23 Highland Scot

24 Mrs. King
26 Rosie of song
29 Russian industrial city
30 Debatable
31 Concealed
32 Network
35 Rev. King's award: 1964
39 Ornamental fish
40 Cordage fiber
41 Dismounted
42 Sails over clouds
43 Civil War battle site
45 Birthplace of Rev.
King

48 Jazzman Getz
49 Reside
50 Meditates
54 Philospher _____-tse
55 Famed words of Rev.
King: Aug. 1963
59 Rhone tributary
60 Speed skater Enke
61 Greene from Ottawa
62 Actress Claire
63 Chosen ones
64 Lyric poem

DOWN

1 Horne in "Stormy
Weather"
2 N.C. college
3 Clue
4 Supporter
5 Pulled up after a canter
6 Serf
7 Thirst quencher
8 Sportscaster Scully
9 NASDAQ term
10 Fills with joy
11 Decalogue verb
12 Washington sound
13 Kingdome is one
18 Like greasepaint
22 Netherlands river

24 "Odyssey" enchantress
25 Wavy, in Orly
26 Prefix for present
27 Virtuous
28 Toga
29 Repasts
31 Ancient capital of
Edom
32 Historian Durant
33 Basso Pinza
34 Golfer Daniel
36 Leonine
37 H.S. test
38 Storm particle
42 _____ ammoniac
43 Portico

44 Manage
45 Ike's opponent at the
polls
46 Finn's creator
47 Soprano Mitchell
48 Worn out
51 Eliel Saarinen's son
52 "The Fountainhead"
author
53 Captain Hook's henchman
56 Cartoonist Foster
57 Hundredth of a hectare
58 London's "Old" theater

87

ACROSS

1 Ariadne's father
4 French historian: 1823–92
11 Show
12 Wed sub rosa
14 Species of narcissus
15 Confidently held
17 "_____ of prevention . . ."
18 Manumit
19 Jacques's beast
20 Votes opposed
22 Put in an appearance
23 Mechanical fasteners
26 Cast a ballot
27 Loci
28 Rich in oxygen
30 Warded off
32 Held fast
35 Shot
39 Lot
40 Gave cheer to one in fear
43 Four gills
44 Nice moon
45 U.S. Govt. agency
46 Firedog
48 Lay
51 City in W Calif.
52 Relinquishments
53 Buddhist maxims
54 Say
55 Signets
56 Measures of time

DOWN

1 Composer of "The Medium"
2 Judicial investigation
3 Word that may be parsed
4 Auricular
5 Luna, to Laodice
6 "_____, go!"
7 Legendary North Pole group
8 Word heard at Yuletide
9 Plum's kin
10 Veined, to a botanist
11 Receivers of gifts
13 Believed
14 Blows in the ring
16 Stowe novel
21 Granted
24 Stop
25 Invitation abbr.
26 "Quo _____?"
29 Court whistlers
31 Uncanny quality
32 Backbones
33 Four-wheeled carriages
34 Adept entertainer
36 Exceed the limits
37 Classroom needs
38 Ariz.'s Painted _____
39 Kin of thermae
41 Jet's route
42 Pops
44 Most common, to statisticians
47 Singer Coolidge
49 Contentment
50 City in Tuscany

88

ACROSS

1 Boys
5 A power source
10 Secure
14 French violinist: 18th century
15 Ling-Ling, e.g.
16 Part of Q.E.D.
17 Notion
18 Norse sagas
19 About: Abbr.
20 Part of a drummer's gear
22 Egyptian monarch
24 West role
25 Metric unit
26 A.S.A.P.
30 Hampers
34 For each
35 Luftwaffe, to R.A.F.
37 Glacial block of ice
38 State or lake
40 Opera hat
42 Prima donna
43 Stoneworker
45 Replacement parts for a cobbler
47 Wax: Comb. form
48 Resins used in varnish
50 Summer beverage
52 Milky gems
54 Anger
55 Part of a signature
58 Everlasting
62 Playing card
63 Vinegary: Comb. form
65 Weathercock
66 First rib-loser
67 Type of type
68 Sicilian volcano
69 Potential blooms
70 Anoint, old style
71 Rise sharply

DOWN

1 Secular
2 Griffith or Williams
3 Judge
4 Nativity site
5 Kind of bee
6 Bits
7 Finish
8 Make suitable
9 Like some hot potatoes
10 Hidden
11 Cherubini creation
12 Gambling game
13 Engrave with acid
21 White House figure
23 Hellenic hawk
25 Emblems
26 Froth
27 Corolla part
28 Expunge
29 Garlands
31 Heath
32 Was delirious
33 Frighten
36 Holiday season
39 This puzzle has three sets of _____
41 Musical half step
44 Palm or liquor
46 Painful
49 Maple fruit
51 Hysteria
53 Ecole assignment
55 Stiletto thrust
56 Indic language
57 Peruse
58 Relative of etc.
59 Defense acronym
60 Ballerina Pavlova
61 He was "every inch a king"
64 Scottish uncle

89

ACROSS

1 Large, thick pieces
6 Cicatrix
10 Expense
14 Chaos
15 Hawaiian island
16 Butter's rival
17 Witch doctor's fetish
18 Secluded spot
19 Plant
20 Panic
22 Varied
24 Entranceway
26 Caper
27 Kneecaps

31 Typical
35 Cargo
36 Chinese weight
38 Yarn
39 Rainbow
40 Spouse's relative
41 Antique
42 "How sweet _____!":
   Gleason
44 African lake
45 Punctilious one
46 Frat brother's activity
48 News-item heading
50 Not so plentiful

52 Siberian river
53 Draftees
57 Liturgy
61 Rant's partner
62 October stone
64 "Beau _____"
65 Gen. Bradley
66 Exploding star
67 Spars
68 Multitudinous
69 Watched
70 Subtle airs

DOWN

1 Injection
2 French poet: 16th
   century
3 Declare
4 Got on
5 Academy
6 Soak, in Yorkshire
7 Serene
8 In the van
9 Modern convenience
10 Solace
11 Mixture
12 Hawk

13 Related
21 Vagabond
23 Altar words
25 Wet
27 Glen _____
28 Main corporeal vessel
29 Implied but unspoken
30 Caesar or Waldorf
32 New Zealand native
33 Spent
34 Shelf
37 Twangy
43 Argentine

45 Ky.'s Pennyroyal, e.g.
47 Teachers' org.
49 Riddle
51 Indian soldier, for-
   merly
53 High-school dance
54 Vishnu incarnation
55 A tsar
56 Redeem
58 Former Union
59 "_____ boy!"
60 _____-majesté
63 Stripling

90

ACROSS

1 Sea dogs
6 Excursion
10 Distinctive time periods
14 Con _____ (lovingly): Mus.
15 Aborigine in Japan
16 Poet Ogden
17 Rabbit
18 "Decameron" author
20 Summer time in Sedan
21 Stream sediment
23 Was overly sweet
24 ICBM or SAM
26 Ananias, e.g.
27 Kind of pad
28 The element carbon, e.g.
32 Empty boasting
36 Robin Hood's drink
37 Be deserving of
38 Señora Perón
39 Historic town NW of Moscow
40 Make do, with "out"
41 Vatican legate
45 Millet subjects
47 Married
48 Shot tosses
49 Essay
53 British martyr-saint
56 Harris's _____ Rabbit
57 Norwegian violinist Bull
58 Tchaikovsky's "_____ Italien"
60 Herbert Hoover, for one
62 Symbol of early March
63 Charged particles
64 Upright
65 Leaf cutters
66 Former Venetian magistrate
67 Challenges

DOWN

1 Ore.'s capital
2 Fine violin
3 Easy paces
4 Three: Prefix
5 Having awareness of
6 Postpone
7 Very funny fellow
8 It often follows Co.
9 "Tosca" composer
10 Bis
11 Risqué
12 Name on a French map
13 Did a farrier's job
19 Where Crockett fell
22 A memorable Chase
25 Vestige
26 Kind of train
28 Variable stars
29 Chalky silicate
30 Others, to Ovid
31 Open-mesh fabric
32 Paging signal
33 Do an autumnal job
34 Neighborhood
35 Govt. divisions
39 Patella site
41 King of Greece: 1947–64
42 Sodium carbonate, e.g.
43 Promise to pay
44 Like a raw recruit
46 Treats contemptuously
49 Came into being
50 Haying machine
51 "Peyton _____"
52 Camps out
53 U.S.C. rival
54 Play featuring Sadie Thompson
55 Type of news or survey
56 Former Met impresario
59 Dovecote sound
61 "_____ pro nobis"

91

ACROSS

1 Opponent
5 Object
10 Stumble
14 Kind of cloth
15 Make the Alpine echoes ring
16 Home of the Baylor Bears
17 Hebrew letter
18 Homeland of Icarus
19 Pizza-parlor necessity
20 Rocket component
22 Hash house
24 Flat or pump
25 Bouffant hairdo
26 "Once _____, twice shy"
29 Puritan
33 Biblical prophet
34 Mar
36 Norse navigator
37 Oahe is one
38 Scandinavian coin
39 Set
40 Bavarian river
42 Window adjunct
44 Story of the Forsytes
45 Small bouquets
47 Curdling agent
49 John Irving protagonist
50 Sino-Tibetan language
51 Consternation
54 Having a snub snout
58 American author: 1909–55
59 Terry or Burstyn
61 Tiny opening
62 Rainbow
63 Heckle
64 Common Lat. catchall
65 Glass
66 Rendezvous
67 Pretty girl

DOWN

1 Actor Arkin
2 _____ contendere
3 Connections
4 Swarms over
5 Magnates
6 Lena or Marilyn
7 _____ fixe (obsession)
8 Hockey item
9 Jubilant
10 Describing some cars
11 Talk unintelligibly
12 Baker's aide
13 Yankee Doodle's mount
21 Guevara
23 "Where the Boys _____," 1961 song
25 E.T. or Starman
26 Spa in Austria
27 Insect stage
28 Heavy literature?
29 Godunov of opera
30 Sing-along instrument
31 Blockade
32 Brilliance
35 Hydra or sea anemone
41 Go back
42 Wimpole Street resident
43 Police ploy
44 Pried
46 Federal watchdog agcy.
48 Suffix for any cardinal point
50 Surmise
51 Greet
52 Legendary monster
53 Restrain
54 Disport
55 Explorer De _____
56 Of an age
57 Farmer's locale, in a song
60 Celtic sea god

92

ACROSS

1 U.S. Army vehicle
5 Chateaubriand tale
9 Body of African warriors
13 Transverse shaft
14 Former P.M. of Israel
15 Short fiber
16 Spoke slightingly
18 _____ out (stall)
19 Letter from Crete
20 Scriptures in Lat.
21 Picasso, at times
23 Set free
25 _____ Sandman of song
28 Tomato blights
32 Mine, in Metz
33 Vessel for heating liquids
35 Double-headed drum
36 Shopping area
37 Italian banking center
39 Some Feds
40 Spreads thin
42 Pts. of aeons
43 Beame and Fortas
44 Ancient city in Asia Minor
46 Orange shade
48 Goes too far
50 Scale
52 One hundred square meters
53 Diamonds, to hoods
56 Paint crudely
57 Heaping dish
60 Seed covering
61 Nixies and pixies
62 Hip
63 Intricate passages
64 Gypsy gentlemen
65 Vienna, to the Viennese

DOWN

1 Nephrite
2 Stage direction
3 Maxwell or Lanchester
4 Go
5 Down-to-earth
6 Humpty Dumpty
7 Family member
8 Bear
9 Minor items
10 Sounds from the barn
11 Half _____ (shrimp)
12 Sort
14 Pieces of burned woodland
17 Biblical name for Heliopolis
22 Gardens
23 Big A event
24 Overlays
25 Parts of doors
26 Town on the Tigris
27 _____ equation
29 Cobra's cousin
30 Emitting smoke
31 Import
34 Comments on a literary work
38 Declares
41 Hindu god of destruction
45 _____ paratus (plea at law)
47 Weapon for Athos
49 Recover
50 Poet Teasdale
51 Short test
53 Territory in SW Morocco
54 Clever
55 N.C. college
56 Hoover, e.g.
58 Hail, to Caesar
59 Brawl

93

ACROSS

1 Freud's "Totem und ____"
5 An O'Neal
10 Its cap. is Pierre
14 Pavlov
15 Rancher's lariat
16 Dock support
17 Auriferous Connery film?
19 "____ Rock" (Simon-Garfunkel song)
20 Approve
21 Billy the Kid, e.g.
23 Snood
24 Urey or Stassen, to Guido
26 Become manifest
29 Fruit of an Asiatic palm
32 Hamlet's cry of distaste
33 Smith and Jackson
35 Whirl
36 "____ Clear Day"
37 T.C.U. rival
38 Compass pt.
41 Once around the track
42 ____ vez (again, to Alfonso)
44 Admit
46 ____ de France
47 Dubious story
50 Sings like a bird
52 Arachnid
53 Prepare leather
54 Lacking pigmentation
56 Pale and worn
60 "America" is a proper one
61 Glowing song-and-dance gal?
64 Gambler's "bones"
65 Wear away
66 Fountain treat
67 Pens
68 Come to fruition
69 Check

DOWN

1 Buster Brown's dog
2 Rugby's river
3 Glabrous
4 Ruined
5 Sterne's "____ Shandy"
6 Eldest, to Yves
7 Children's game
8 Shoshonean
9 Actress Kidder
10 Lathe part
11 Sparkling West role?
12 Woman in "Summer and Smoke"
13 Sartre work
18 Crotchets
22 Rubber tree
24 Actor Vigoda
25 Correct a watch
26 On the move
27 A 1492 caravel
28 "The Good Earth" was one of her gems
30 J.F.K.'s Sec. of the Interior
31 Sorts
34 Fabric named after a French city
39 Frost's "The Road ____"
40 Madden
43 Goats, butterflies or plants
45 Always, in poesy
48 Container
49 Crèche figure
51 Swallow
54 "The King ____"
55 Cut of meat
56 ____ Park, birthplace of F.D.R.
57 Medicinal plant
58 Beatty film
59 Mild oath
62 Psychic Geller
63 Jazz form

94

ACROSS

1 Roman conspirator
7 Partner of 1 Across
14 Tebaldi and Scotto
16 Triple _____: 1907–17
17 Plain
18 Storyteller
19 Douceur
20 Italian saint
22 D.C. ecology group
23 Wang Lung's wife
25 Cather's "_____ Lady"
26 Piquancy
27 A fiddler and a pianist
29 "Hamlet" part
30 Very, to Verdi
32 Pub game
34 Encourages
36 What a cicerone conducts
38 Director De _____
39 Taught
43 Mercury, e.g.
46 Lend _____ (aid)
47 Mail convenience: Abbr.
49 Thomas's "_____ Go Gentle . . ."
51 Thing, to Tacitus
52 Cougars
54 Recherché
55 This, in Paris
56 Silver-eagle wearer
58 Org. fostering opera, etc.
59 Van Gogh's "Room _____"
61 Believes
63 Cloy
64 Wind
65 March 15
66 Victim on 65 Across

DOWN

1 A founder of Surrealism
2 Vilipended
3 A woman who has borne one child
4 Dramatist Mosel
5 Salt Lake City team
6 Bag man
7 Horned viper
8 Concerning
9 Manche's capital
10 Celebes or China
11 Considerable
12 Idealist
13 Jones's prize in 1779
15 Pillarlike monument
21 Marshal of France in W.W. I
24 Carney role in "The Honeymooners"
28 Tolerated
30 Followed a curving course
31 Turbine part
33 Rio Grande do _____, Brazil
35 Object
37 Disgusts
39 Caustic wit
40 Swift cat
41 Arrow-shaped
42 Major-_____
44 Biblical fibber
45 Singer Lynn
48 Judges' seats
50 Ecdysiast, e.g.
52 Rostand or Ronsard
53 Silken
56 Draped, e.g.
57 Miss Genst?
60 Venezia's canals
62 Proper

95

ACROSS

1 Mount in the Cascade Range
7 Break a fast
10 Spanish landlady
13 Aide
14 Puts in a setting
16 Like the Earth's shape
17 Book after Ezra
18 Disaccustom
19 Neighbor of Bol.
21 Compact
22 Shoe part
25 Pelagic predators
26 Entertain
29 Chinese, in Roma
31 Former Turkish officials
33 B.&O. depot
34 Masticate
38 Table spread
39 Hate
41 Verdi heroine
42 Campus bldg.
43 School of whales
44 Cater basely
46 Entrance to Hades
49 Ship's upward heaving
50 Alone
52 Workers' org.
54 Breathing problems
56 Memo heading
57 Fatty's problem
61 Deli offering
63 Clarify
65 "_____ Deadly Sins": Weill
66 Grippers for the Gipper
67 Pose
68 Word with lap or drop
69 Lacquer ingredients

DOWN

1 Display
2 Cupbearer on Olympus
3 Actress Nazimova
4 Fluffy dishes
5 Eastern holiday
6 Regions
7 Memphis-to-Knoxville dir.
8 After sieben
9 "_____ rosemary . . .": Ophelia
10 Meccawee, e.g.
11 Protein providers
12 Pallid
14 Breakfast treat
15 _____ bean (a Ky. tree)
20 Fabulous bird
23 Govt. sponsor of opera, etc.
24 Within: Comb. form
26 Footless
27 Hawaiian loincloth
28 Addict
30 Crabbe role: 1958
32 Wise one
35 Skin
36 Nod neighbor
37 Turn aside, with "off"
40 Slavic nurse
45 "_____ Lay Dying": Faulkner
47 Emulated Simba
48 Like Renard
50 Turkish cavalryman
51 Beginning
53 "Odyssey" enchantress
54 Bldg. units
55 Except
58 Author O'Flaherty
59 Oppositionist
60 Mrs. Truman
62 European gull
64 Wright wing

ACROSS

1 Atlas contents
5 Excuse
10 Stain
14 Inter _____
15 Unstable particle
16 S.A. rodent
17 Radio-comics character
20 Annapolis graduates
21 Jungle queen
22 _____ Speedwagon (rock group)
23 Lachrymal drop
24 City on the Rhone
27 Sun. talk
28 Beethoven's "_____ Solemnis"
33 Bishop's seat
34 "Ode on a Grecian _____"
35 Collar lining
36 Early Claude Rains film
40 Blonde bombshell of the 30's
41 April 13, in Italy
42 Victoria's "We _____ not amused"
43 TV hillbilly
44 Crazy Horse, to Custer
45 Fastener
47 Bus.-school course
49 Afternoon reception
50 Eight-sided figure
54 Distorts reports
58 Frankie Frisch
60 Informal goodbye
61 Size of type
62 Within: Comb. form
63 _____-Neisse Line
64 Jewish feast
65 Profound

DOWN

1 Spiked club
2 King of comedy
3 Gladys Knight's backups
4 Caricature
5 _____ acids
6 Optical glass
7 Doctrine
8 Heating tank
9 Gandhi's land
10 Rotate
11 Youthful attendant
12 Newspaper publisher: 1858–1935
13 Makes lace
18 Matures
19 Usual
23 Tautness
24 _____ crow flies
25 G.I. therapy
26 Salacious looks
27 _____ Lanka
29 What Eliza crossed
30 Flowing robe
31 Trap
32 Vice President before Ford
34 Alphabetic trio
35 G-men's org.
37 _____ du Diable
38 External world
39 Fish or suffix
44 Caress
45 Slave of yore
46 Sent by wire
48 Pearmain centers
49 More insipid
50 Hahn or Kahn
51 Libyan neighbor
52 Pierre's head
53 At a distance
54 Ball-park figure
55 Narrow way
56 Padua neighbor
57 Store
59 Stashed away

97

ACROSS

1 Ukrainian saint
5 Fossil resin
10 City on the Jumna
14 Meager
15 Guileless
16 Percolate
17 Expressed regrets
19 Inflection
20 Poe's lost maiden
21 Marked by misfortune
23 Expression of sorrow
26 Eager
27 Gen. MacArthur's companion
32 And so forth: Abbr.
35 Profit
36 Coffee containers
37 _____ Minor
38 Reveille instrument
39 Pose
40 Clutches
41 Wings for Amor
42 List of choices
43 Former Broadway hit
44 NASA vehicle's unit
45 Gallic gala
47 Russia's _____ Industrial Area
49 Proofreader's word
50 Velasquez subject
53 Outburst
58 Float
59 Haiti and the Dominican Republic
62 French girlfriend
63 Alliance
64 Related
65 Post
66 First British settlement in India
67 Hazard

DOWN

1 Iridescent gem
2 Run easily
3 Segar's Alice
4 Woody's son
5 _____ State University, Tex.
6 Juin predecessor
7 Show _____
8 Twain's "_____ Diary"
9 Railway porters
10 Houston player
11 Author of "Indiana"
12 Clair or Coty
13 Imitated
18 Delphi resident
22 Mature
24 Maltreats
25 Dashes
27 Plot
28 Small egg
29 Tatterdemalion
30 Longest river
31 Understand innately
33 Leg bone
34 One of the Jones boys
37 Composer of "Rule, Britannia"
40 Founder of eugenics
42 Population-study pioneer
45 Forbid
46 Syria, Lebanon and neighbors
48 Judged
50 Retirement funds, for short
51 Appoint
52 Hokkaido aborigine
54 Pinocchio, e.g.
55 Father of the Midgard serpent
56 Some Ivy Leaguers
57 Sudden pull
60 Title for a baronet
61 Ky. bluegrass

98

ACROSS

1 Brief breath
5 Palm off
10 Shortcoming
14 Second of a Latin trio
15 Forster's "A Passage to _____"
16 Inauguration ritual
17 Reek
18 Saltations
19 Tom Joad, e.g.
20 Decoration
22 Two-point football score
24 Old salt
25 Cherubini product
27 Sculls
29 Panicky
33 Noncom rank
36 Indigent
38 Thick woolen fabric
39 Magician's expression
41 "The _____ jealousy heareth all things": Apocrypha
43 "As you _____"
44 Semirural region
46 _____ T. Firefly, Groucho role
48 Atrabilious
49 Make reparation
51 Possible prince
53 Madrid museum
55 Tex. river
59 Milquetoast
62 Decoration
64 Wheel connection
65 Bottom-line figure
67 Both: Comb. form
68 Dread
69 "You _____ Fair," 1937 song
70 Footnote abbr.
71 Up-tight
72 Take up again
73 D.C. nine once in the A.L.

DOWN

1 Spars
2 Stubborn as _____
3 Pacific island group
4 False
5 Decoration
6 Numerical openers
7 The Gem State
8 Drink a little
9 Mortarboard decoration
10 Decoration
11 Geneva or Constance
12 Keep _____ (persevere)
13 Muffet fare
21 Horse color
23 Kuwaiti resident
26 Boodle
28 Desiccated
30 Architect _____ van der Rohe
31 Pound, the poet
32 Turn
33 Graf von _____
34 Comedian Redd
35 Brilliant stroke
37 Actress Joanne
40 Ostentation
42 Decoration
45 Negri contemporary
47 Put in order
50 Dental calculus
52 Arthur's nephew
54 Time after time
56 City in S Malawi
57 Glenn's path in 1962
58 Hit the _____ (fail)
59 Bistro
60 Fired
61 Cinder
63 Make an incised mark
66 Pay dirt

99

ACROSS

1 Tamworths
5 Type of energy
10 Limited
12 Tommyrot!
14 Submissive
15 ". . . that _____ religion"
16 Power agcy.
17 R.N.'s dispensations
19 Backyard sport
20 Grate
22 Suction-pipe strainer
23 Lockup
24 Idolize
26 Bad _____, German spa
27 Shades of brown
28 Gymnasium
30 Cross preceder
31 Is conspicuous
33 Celerity
35 Hoosier
39 Bridges
40 Stout
41 A daughter of Dione
42 Former Baltimorean
43 Type of lace
45 Protuberance
46 Maple seed's wing
47 Actor in "The Green Berets"
49 Accomplished
50 Buff
52 Puts up fodder
54 Made tough
55 Inventor Rudolf
56 Perfume ingredient
57 Ladies of Sp.

DOWN

1 Sunshade
2 Nickname for Thalberg
3 Storage-battery plate
4 Concert performances
5 Beaver State's capital
6 Automobile pioneer
7 Garonne tributary
8 Grieg's "_____ Dance"
9 Lasts
10 The Sagebrush State
11 Occidental
12 Counterfeit
13 Safecrackers
14 Wristlet
18 Tatouay or tatou
21 Accounted for
23 Part of Elizabeth II's realm
25 Billie Sol _____
27 Cub, e.g.
29 Little fellow
30 Adult scrod
32 Displayed disdain
33 Italian olive-growing center
34 Idle chatter
36 Explores an idea
37 Milton's "servant of God"
38 The basics
39 Lots and lots
40 Forwarded
43 Makes an escape
44 Ancient city of Egypt
47 Huns' king
48 River into the North Sea
51 _____ hill 'n' dale
53 "The law _____ ass": Dickens

100

ACROSS

1 Gaff
5 An N.C.O.
9 Nobelist Bellow
13 Dover _____
14 Sourpuss
16 Aqua _____
17 Spot for a Turkish bath
19 Entrance for Clementine's dad
20 Milady's interest
21 Any Pelican State county
23 Convince
24 "Experientia _____"
25 Diamond part
28 "Madama Butterfly" props
31 Ancient Armenia
33 "You can bet _____!"
34 Saw with the grain
35 Having finesse
36 Japanese verse form
38 Realty investment
39 Chemical suffix
40 Soccer great
41 Due; payable
43 Full
45 "A Boy _____ Sue"
46 Eared seal
47 Rabbit or Fox
49 "_____-Boom-De-Ré"
51 Empty talk
54 Deep blue
55 Stoppage of activity
58 Case for trivia
59 Retired Met soprano
60 To be, to Baudelaire
61 Himalayan holy man
62 It might be light
63 Enthusiastic

DOWN

1 Draft initials
2 Ottoman
3 Actor-director Alan
4 State anew
5 Overindulge
6 Flynn of filmdom
7 Knock into a cocked hat
8 Kokoon
9 Consolations for Mark Roth
10 Kin of an aula
11 "Battle Cry" author
12 Trellis piece
15 Mart
18 Greeks' "unlucky" letter
22 No room to swing _____
24 Moist and chilly
25 Loses color
26 Atlanta's Omni, e.g.
27 Dual-purpose room in a school
28 Jabbed
29 Poisonous Chilean shrub
30 Exceed 55 m.p.h.
32 Chaplin short
37 Composer Speaks
38 Shatner-Nimoy vehicle
40 He wrote "I Kid You Not"
42 Highest of the Pyrenees
44 Where Firenze is
47 Pair
48 Assessor
49 Weight of E Asia
50 B'way group
51 _____-dieu (kneeling bench)
52 Mineral: Comb. form
53 River at Chartres
56 Earth is one
57 Pawns and knights, e.g.

ANSWERS

1

```
VALID NOEL  OMAR
AMUSEMENTS  FORA
ABRAHAMANDISAAC
LIE ARENA  NINNY
    DATA    SHA
OATES   ALHAMBRA
HIRE  KOREAN  AUX
ADAMCAINANDABEL
RES  ARLENE  MEDE
ASHTRAYS   COLES
    ITT   ALAN
AMORE  KAROL  ALI
DAVIDANDSOLOMON
OPEN  LEVITATION
SARG  BETS  STEPS
```

2

```
PELF  SATIN  REFS
ODOR  CLOSE  ELLA
TARO  OONAS  GUAM
 MENOFFEWWORDS
   TAFT     PEEK
 AIRS    VALET
ECTO  REASON  DUO
THEWEIRDSISTERS
EER  DONETS  IAGO
   NITER   ANNE
 OPEC     PINS
 ARETHEBESTMEN
ARID  EMILE  ICON
SELL  AMEER  THEE
IDLE  RAREE  HOLE
```

3

```
 RAF  CLAMP  PICA
HELL  RADII  HALE
OTTO  ARECA  IGOR
ORATING  ANALOGY
FORSAKE    ILL
   AMY  PASTIMES
CLIMB  JUXTAPOSE
AES   PALES   ASP
PALISADES  BENET
ENAMELED  BOA
    PRE  QUARTET
STREETS  ARTLESS
TOUR  OUSTS  DATA
OMNI  TREAT  OMER
PEEL  SEARS  MSS
```

4

```
SCRAPS   RELATE
ALABAMA  KARELIA
VAPORED  RINGERS
ERI  TADPOLE  WAT
REDS  RUINS  BIDE
STATE  CEE  FIFER
 SNEEZE  RHODES
   ARE    OLD
 TORIES  ADDICT
MARIE  HUR  SNORT
ERIN  SEPIA  GROW
SAN  SEASONS  STE
SNOOPER  SEAGATE
ETCHERS  ENGAGED
ROOSTS   TOPERS
```

211

5

```
E A S E . . P I A . R A N G
C L E A . T U R K S . O P A L
H E A R T B R E A K H O U S E
O C T . R A P S . O U T R A N
. . . G I R L . P A R S E .
. P H R A S E . O L D . H E S
P L A I D . H E N . S E N T
L A S T S . E N D . S T A V E
A N T S . . A G E . T A R O T
T E Y . D E R . R A R I T Y
. . H A U N T . H U E D .
O B E Y E D . S E T A . B E A
H E A R T O F D A R K N E S S
T A R E . W E A R Y . A L A S
O R T S . . M K T . G L U T
```

6

```
. P O R T . D A R E . H A R P
M O T O R . E L E V . A L E E
A N I T A . P U R E . S A N E
D E C O N T A M I N A T I O N
. . . . C A R . T I E . . .
C O N T E N T I O U S N E S S
O B E Y . . B R A E . N A P
W O V E . B A S E L . H A L E
E L I . S U R E . E T O N
D I S E N T A N G L E M E N T
. . L A C . O A S . . .
U N S O P H I S T I C A T E D
R E A P . E R A T . A G A V E
S A K E . R A G E . R E N E W
A R I D . S E A N . P E G S .
```

7

```
D E M I . P E S T . P A S H A
A T O M . E V E R . A S P E N
D R O M E D A R Y . T H E R E
S E R E N A D E . S I E N N A
. . . D O L E . S P E N S E R
C H A I S E . S H U N . .
L O M A . R E P E R T O I R E
E M I T . L E A . B R O W
F O R E A N D A F T . S A T E
. . R E E K . A R E N A S
E M P E R O R . A V E S .
L E A V E N . P H E A S A N T
M A R I S . G U E R R I L L A
E D I C T . O R A N . O A R S
R E S T S . B E D S . N I B S
```

8

```
A M A T I . L A S S . P R A Y
D E M O B . A L O P . R U S E
A N I L E . C A L E D O N I A
S U N D R I E S . C O P T E R
. . . . I N D . A I L . .
. D A M A S . A N A T O L I A
P A L O . A R I L . R E N D
O L I O . C R E S S . D A L E
S A M S . O R N E . E V E N
H I B E R N I A . E G R E T
. . . A S S . S E A . .
P A T E N T . D E C L A I M S
A Q U I T A N I A . L I C I T
T U R N . N O R M . I R E N A
H A K E . T H E Y . A S S E T
```

9

```
T A B S · R E A R · · S P A N
A C A T · E R S E · S H O N E
R I T E · V A S E · C A N T O
A D H E R E S · F R A N C E S
· · S P A R E S · I N K E D ·
S P H E R E · T E N S E · ·
T H E R E · S E A S · D A R K
E B B · R O T A T E D · G A I
T S A R · M E M S · A D A M S
· · A C A R E · S L U M P S
· A L L A H · R E C A N E ·
S T E L L A R · T H I N M A N
T R A I L · O C H O · I N G E
A I D E S · O L E O · N O R A
B A S S · · F U L L · G N A T
```

10

```
M A L T A · R A S A · L A I C
I L I A C · E L A M · A C R E
S M E L T · B E W I T C H E D
C A U C U S E S · C H E E S E
· · A R C · W A R · · ·
· A S T R O · R E B O U N D S
A L L O Y · A L L E L U I A
G O I N · M O N T E · T I D Y
E N T I C I N G · A R T I S
R E S O U R C E · B L A S T
· R T E · A L I · · ·
A F L A S H · C A U C A S U S
G R A D E F O U R · I N O N E
O O Z E · U P T O · A O S T A
G M E N · L E A N · S N O O T
```

11

```
T O D A Y · J O G · H E A D
O R A T E · O N E S · A N D A
R E Y E S · Y E S T E R D A Y
I S L A M · S A T U R D A Y S
· A R E S · D E N S · ·
L A B · N A S A · G A S C O N
E R O S · G O Y A · T E A S E
A E R O B E S · G A Z E L L E
S T E L A · O D E S · S L E D
H E R A L D · A R E A · I R S
· L A D Y · A M A T · ·
O N E D A Y A T A · A D A P T
H O L I D A Y O N · N A D I R
I R I S · T I N A · D R A P E
O M S K · N A T · A S Y E T
```

12

```
F L A T · R E G A L · S P A R
L I R A · E R A S E · H A R I
A M E R I G O V E S P U C C I
N E A P T I D E · S A N T A S
· H O E · L E S T · ·
S E A M A N · P E N T · H A J
A N T I C · M A T E · S O L O
V A L L A D O L I D S P A I N
E T A L · E T O N · A U R A E
D E S · S T E S · P I N E R S
· L A O S · H A L · ·
R E T U R N · G E N O V E S E
I T A L I A N A M E R I C A N
A N I L · T A M I L · T O L D
S A L S · E G A N S · A N T S
```

13

P	A	C	T		R	F	D			M	A	T	C	H
A	L	A	S		E	L	A	S		I	D	A	H	O
N	O	M	E		L	U	M	P		N	O	T	E	D
G	N	P		P	A	M	P	A	S	G	R	A	S	S
	E	F	F	A	C	E		R	U	L	E	R	S	
	I	O	L	E		S	T	E	E	D				
T	E	R	R	E		L	A	D	S			T	I	N
A	L	E	M		S	T	O	N	E		P	A	N	E
T	I	S		S	I	R	E			N	O	M	A	D
	L	I	N	U	S		P	E	E	P				
	D	O	O	D	A	D		O	R	A	T	E	S	
L	A	M	P	L	I	G	H	T	E	R		R	O	T
E	T	A	P	E		E	A	T	S		N	I	N	O
E	T	H	E	R		S	T	E	T		E	N	I	D
R	O	A	D	S			S	R	O		E	G	A	D

14

S	O	D	A		B	A	L	E	S			R	A	C	E
E	L	A	N		O	G	I	V	E			A	D	I	T
T	I	R	E		N	A	D	E	R			R	I	D	E
	O	N	C	E	U	P	O	N	A	T	I	M	E		
	D	O	S	E							I	T	E	R	
S	C	I	O	N			H	A	S	T	Y				
P	A	N	T		S	P	I	R	A	L		D	A	P	
O	N	C	E	I	N	A	L	I	F	E	T	I	M	E	
T	E	A		R	A	T	T	L	E		E	V	I	L	
	R	A	G	E	S			G	R	A	D	E			
D	I	E	T			O	M	A	R						
	O	N	C	E	A	N	D	F	O	R	A	L	L		
C	R	E	E		S	E	A	T	S		P	O	O	H	
B	I	R	D		P	A	L	E	S		I	N	G	E	
S	A	T	E		S	P	I	N	Y		N	E	O	N	

15

S	L	A	B		G	A	O	L		A	B	A	T	E
C	O	C	O		A	M	M	O		C	O	L	O	N
O	C	H	S		R	E	N	O		E	X	T	R	A
T	H	E	C	O	R	N	I	S	G	R	E	E	N	
	B	E	D			A	B	S						
L	I	O	N	E	T		E	L	M			S	S	W
O	S	T	I	A		E	M	E	U		W	E	A	R
C	A	T	C	H	E	R	I	N	T	H	E	R	Y	E
A	W	E	E		V	O	L	T		A	L	V	I	N
L	A	R		A	S	S		I	S	L	E	T	S	
	B	A	N			A	T	T						
	B	E	A	N	S	A	N	D	B	A	R	L	E	Y
B	E	A	R	S		C	O	D	A		O	O	Z	E
L	A	R	G	E		E	P	I	C		S	O	R	A
E	D	S	E	L		D	E	S	K		A	M	A	H

16

K	O	P	S		S	A	H	I	B		O	G	R	E
E	L	L	A		O	P	E	R	A		C	R	A	W
P	L	A	Y	B	Y	P	L	A	Y		H	A	Z	E
T	A	Y		T	A	E	L		H	O	R	N	E	R
	I	O	U		A	C	E		B	E	D			
C	O	N	S		P	L	A	Y	P	O	S	S	U	M
O	L	G	A		O	S	T	E	A	L		T	I	E
M	E	T	R	O	S			T	I	T	A	N	S	
B	A	H		S	I	S	A	L	S		A	N	T	S
O	N	E	A	C	T	P	L	A	Y		D	D	A	Y
	F	R	A		A	L	P		A	S	P			
S	K	I	I	N	G		U	S	E	R		L	E	T
T	O	E	S		U	N	D	E	R	P	L	A	Y	S
E	L	L	E		L	E	E	R	S		E	Y	R	A
P	A	D	S		P	A	S	S	E		I	S	E	R

17

```
MOAB . SEWN . ABBA
YALE . THREE . FERN
THEECHOINGGREEN
HUE . OILED . RIFLE
. . SINE . SEC . .
PURPLEMOUNTAIN
ASIA . . PLEA . NUB
DUAD . CHIME . JUDO
SAT . COIN . ARGO
. LAVENDERSGREEN
. . INK . ICAL .
BUILT . SABOT . YAK
ONCEINABLUEMOON
ODES . EMBER . DRNO
PORT . BEET . SKEW
```

18

```
HINT . ASIS . AFREE
ASEA . HOWE . ROOST
NEWT . AJAR . TRUTH
DREAM . ONER . ETES
SELMA . UTTERS . .
. INERT . BEATLE
SOB . TENON . VIRAL
PROFILE . AMELITA
ATOLL . RATER . GEM
TAMALE . UTHER . .
. XANADU . NEVER
ACTS . STIR . DEERE
CRIER . ATNO . FROG
HALEY . LOEW . EDDA
SWEDE . ERRS . RIEN
```

19

```
CAPE . COMIC . SMIT
OVER . OVULE . AIRE
PERRYMASON . TSAR
EST . EELS . TERSER
. BARS . HIRAM .
PAPERS . SAMSPADE
ETHAN . BERET . ROD
LOIN . PORTS . APSE
ELL . SLOGS . ALLEN
ELONGATE . PLIERS
. VETCH . ROOT .
PRAISE . SETH . ALE
HONG . MIKEHAMMER
OUCH . ARISE . OMNI
TEES . TAPER . BOON
```

20

```
DADS . ALAI . MURK
EQUI . GLINT . ASEA
BUTTERANDEGGMAN
SAY . ZESTY . UNCLE
. . TREK . ARE . .
. BREADANDBUTTER
LAIC . AILS . AMI
AYAH . PROXY . CHEF
MON . ROAM . AONE
BUTTERFINGERED .
. APE . EAST . .
BASTE . TAXIS . ASA
LITTLEBUTTERCUP
OREL . GANTS . UTES
TYPE . ORTO . GAZE
```

21

```
H E L D ■ A P A R T ■ I S M S
E R I E ■ C R I E R ■ N O A H
M I M I ■ T E R S E ■ H A R E
S C A R V E S ■ T A P E R E D
■ ■ D I S T O R T E R ■ ■
S N A R L ■ O B I ■ R I A T A
M O T E L S ■ S C A T T E R S
U F O ■ A H A ■ T W I ■ G I S
T A N A G E R S ■ E N C I N A
S T E V E ■ T A R ■ E A S E D
■ A R M E N I A N S ■
A D V I S O R ■ O C T A V O S
R I A L ■ P I E T A ■ B E D E
C A N E ■ E A V E S ■ A G E E
S L E D ■ S L A D E ■ S A R D
```

22

```
B O A S T S ■ P T A ■ O A S T
A T M O S T ■ E R S ■ D U P E
S H I P P E D O U T ■ E T R E
S O D S ■ P E N M A N S H I P
■ T I A R A ■ O N E
I T S A ■ K E E N ■ V E R G E
S H I P P E R S ■ T I A S ■
R E S H I P S ■ T H E S H I P
■ T I N T ■ D O E S T I M E
C R E D O ■ A I R Y ■ S P A T
O E R ■ L A S E R ■
M A S T E R S H I P ■ A P R A
E C H O ■ L E A D E R S H I P
S T I R ■ E R R ■ N A T I V E
A S P S ■ S T D ■ D E A L E R
```

23

```
G R O G ■ S A L I C ■ S L A P
Y O U R ■ A M A R A ■ T O D O
M I C E ■ F A V O R ■ O T I S
■ S H A K E H A N D S W I T H
■ T O T S ■ I R E ■
M I S L A Y ■ A L G A ■ R A W
I D E A L ■ A R E A ■ A I R E
D A R K A N D H A N D S O M E
G H E E ■ O R A D ■ O P T E D
E O S ■ F R A T ■ A R I S E S
■ A U S ■ S T I R ■
H A N D L E W I T H C A R E
O V A L ■ M I T R E ■ T A L L
L E N I ■ A R S O N ■ E M M A
D R A B ■ N E A P S ■ D I O R
```

24

```
P S I S ■ A B L E ■ S A L T S
A T M E ■ F O A M ■ U B O A T
P U P P Y L O V E ■ N E V E R
U F O ■ P A P E R E D ■ I L S
A F F I R M ■ Y E A R N ■
■ T E E T H ■ R E A G A N
A L A S ■ R O T I ■ S C I O
I D O L ■ M A R I E ■ P U R R
L E V I ■ A P S E ■ N I P S
K N E A D S ■ A R S O N ■
■ S N E A K ■ C I G A R S
P O E ■ R I A L T O S ■ M A T
A L A R M ■ F O R T Y L O V E
A L T A I ■ I N I T ■ T R E E
R A S E S ■ R E P S ■ R E N D
```

25

```
 H A P   P I L E   L O R C A
M I M I   A V E R   O N I O N
A G O G   R I N G   R A T I O
W H I S T L E D O W N   A N N
      W O O D     R A W
H I T H E R   C R A S H E R S
O R R I S   T R O T   I L E T
M A E S   B O O T H   S I T E
E T A T   A P S O   S T O R E
R E D L I N E S   S A L T O N
      E N T     T A R E
S C I   J U S T W H I S T L E
C O R F U   A R E A   T O O T
A D A I R   L E E R   O G R E
M A N G Y   E S T A   P O D
```

26

```
P A T H   S A L A D   S C A R
A R E A   E L O G E   A R I A
S C A R L E T T A N A G E R S
T A M P E R   T I R E D
O D E O N   C R E M E   E A T
R E D     C O O     O N C E
    S H A M U S   P A C E D
  S C A R L E T L E T T E R
G A O L S   T I A R A S
O G L E     N N E     P A P
B A L   C A R E T   A R O S E
    A P A R A   A D A P T S
A S T U D Y I N S C A R L E T
R E E L   A S C O T   E A R L
C E D E   N E O N S   E R S E
```

27

```
O P A L   T O G A S   S N O W
D E L I   A N I L E   T I D E
S L A T   M I R E D   A L O T
  F R E D A N D G I N G E R
    R I L E S   T E E
E S C A P E   M I A S M A S
L O O T   A M O O N   A R T
F L Y I N G D O W N T O R I O
I V E   A L D E N   U N A U
N E R U D A S   D E T E S T
    N I D   C O R E S
  E D W A R D E H O R T O N
B L U R   A U D I O   R I O T
A S E A   G N A R L   I S L E
H E L P   S A R A S   P E O N
```

28

```
C O N E   B A D E   S O D A
E V E R   B E T E L   K R A N
D A W N S E A R L Y L I G H T
E L S   E R N I E   A I S L E
      A N T I   S Y N
  N O R T H E R N L I G H T S
H E W N   I C A N   E O N
A G I O   P I V O T   N I N A
U R N   S U R E   A D I P
L I G H T F A N T A S T I C
    A E F   W E A L
C A I R N   S T E R N   S A D
O N C E O V E R L I G H T L Y
L O O M   A G A V E   E L A N
E N N S   T O M E   N O S E
```

29

```
PAIL . HOPI . . BAMA
ACRE . ORAD . FADES
CHINAWARE . LAIRS
TESSIE . SABA . EYE
. HEM . POLEVAULT
BOSS . CAISSON .
ACT . ALL . HUTCH
THEMARE . HORIZON
. SWEET . SUN . ERA
. . TREEPIE . SCAB
BRAZILNUT . BAH
LAR . ASIR . TINMAN
ANNUL . GREATDANE
COILS . MEND . ETNA
KNEE . . ADDS . DEER
```

30

```
ARMY . CAROL . SLAY
BEAU . ADORE . PANE
CARLSBADCAVERNS
SPY . HAMS . PACKET
. MEANS . IFNI
AMANDA . FORCEFUL
LARDY . CANOE . IRA
OUTS . RENIG . EGGS
AMI . HOSEA . BLUES
FANTASTS . HAIRDO
. ELSA . TASSE .
TAMALE . EONS . HEW
SLAPSTICKCOMEDY
PALO . TEHEE . CAGE
SILT . IRONS . IDES
```

31

```
ALEC . CASED . SALK
DINE . ORATE . ERIE
ANIL . STRUM . ACME
MODESTYDIEDWHEN
. BOA . TOE .
FIDELIO . RECEDED
OBIS . NIGER . DELI
SSE . LIV . MIT
SETH . RESET . LOOT
ENSURER . TORONTO
. SAL . RUM .
CLOTHESWEREBORN
HURL . ALATE . ABIE
OGLE . SALON . ROTE
PEER . EVENT . DEAR
```

32

```
GIFT . WHAT . MASH
OBIE . SAUCE . ALTI
YELLOWBRICKROAD
AXE . MEADS . NOTRE
. SIPS . TOO .
PAINTTHETOWNRED
ILSA . PAWN . ADE
LISP . WOODY . ANDA
OSU . KIDD . MEIR
THEGOLDENFLEECE
. APE . ILEX .
OUTRE . COCOA . GAB
CLOCKWORKORANGE
TARO . SPEED . CARL
ANON . WELL . ETAL
```

33

```
B A J A ■ D A M P S ■ C O A L
E V E N ■ E N E R O ■ O R L Y
S E R E ■ C O L E P O R T E R
T R O M B O N E S ■ B O S S A
■ M O L D ■ E S S E N ■ ■
A V E N U E S ■ R E S A L E S
B I K E R ■ T H O L E ■ O L E
E T E S ■ P R O O F ■ F R E E
A R R ■ P R I S M ■ F L E C K
M O N S O O N ■ S I L E N T S
■ C R A G S ■ R I T Z ■
S T E A K ■ B E W I T C H E D
S A M M Y D A V I S ■ H A L O
G R I P ■ I S E R E ■ E R S E
T O T S ■ E S N E S ■ R T E S
```

34

```
A B U T ■ B A S R A ■ P A R S
C A V E ■ E L L A S ■ A L A I
T H E R I T E O F S P R I N G
S T A R R I N G ■ E A T I N
■ A I D E ■ R O O D ■ ■
E L A P S E ■ T E M P E R E D
A U R I ■ E A S E L ■ O R O
S T A N D O N C E R E M O N Y
E E R ■ O N O I T ■ A M I E
D R A W N O U T ■ L A R S E N
■ I N R E ■ C A N T ■
I S T L E ■ S E N T I N E L
T H E B R I D A L C A N O P Y
S I T U ■ M E R L E ■ E D E N
A V E R ■ P R I O R ■ T E E N
```

35

```
A T T ■ B U S T S ■ S P A D
D O U R ■ A S T R O ■ T A B U
L Y R E ■ S N A I L P A C E D
I O T A ■ N A V I G A T E
B U L L F I D D L E S ■
■ E M E R Y ■ D A S H E R
C A N ■ M O N E T ■ N A O M I
A G E R ■ N E A R S ■ P R I M
L U C I A ■ S T E E P ■ S T E
M E K O N G ■ A T R E E
■ G O T O T H E D O G S
A P P A L L E D ■ U P O N
G O O S E F L E S H ■ C E D E
A U K S ■ E L O P E ■ E R L E
S T E T ■ R A N T S ■ A Y R
```

36

```
W A S H ■ F L E A ■ S L A M
A C T A ■ M E A N T ■ P O L O
F R O M H A N D T O M O U T H
T E A ■ A N D E S ■ I N D I O
■ S H O E ■ E N G ■
A L L H A N D S O N D E C K
L E E R ■ W A V Y ■ H I P
A N T I ■ H O A R Y ■ D I N E
S T U ■ S A R I ■ A L G A
■ O P E N H A N D E D N E S S
■ L O N ■ I D E A ■
C A R E W ■ O S A G E ■ V I A
H E A V Y H A N D E D N E S S
A R N E ■ S T E E D ■ A L I T
R O A N ■ T H E M ■ E D N A
```

37

```
A L B S   D U M A S   C H A P
M E O W   I N A N E   H A L O
B A B E   O M I N A   I S E E
I N F E R N A L   W A M P U M
  E T O N S   P A L E S T
W I L L I E K E E L E R
H O L Y       W E L F A R E S
A T E   S T I R S     E T H
M A R A T H O N     A F R O
    G E O R G E S I S L E R
  S T A R R Y   R E E S E
S P R I N T   C O R S I C A N
I R O N   A M A T I   S T L O
G E T S   G E N I E   T O I L
N E S T   E X E C S   S R T A
```

38

```
C L O D   G W E N   C R I M E
H O L O   R O B E   H A G A R
E L E C T I O N S   A R O S E
R A G T I M E   T A M E R S
    O N E R S   M O S
S N A R E S   C A P I T A L S
C O R E D   C A L L S   L A C
A R I D   G U L L Y   D I V A
M M E   L O L L S   R O V E R
P A L O A L T O   L A C E R Y
    R T E   P L A I T
  F A T I M A   I N T O N E S
H A R E M   E L E C T R O N S
A D A G E   R A T E   O M I T
T E L A R   O D O R   W E D S
```

39

```
S T A I R S     B R A S S
H A S T E N S   R O A S T E D
O C T A V I A   A N T H O N Y
R I O   S P L I C E S   R A N
E T R E   E I D E R   D A T A
S U I T E   N O R   C A G E S
  S A H A R A   S O O N E S T
    I S O     H A G
C O N C E I T   M O S L E M
I D E A L   A M O   T E L A R
S O U L   S P A R E   R A T A
C A R   O H I O A N S   M I V
O C O N N O R   S A L T I N E
S E N E C A S   S C O O T E R
  R E P E L   T E P E E S
```

40

```
A S H   R A T E D   C O N
R I E L   E L O P E   P A L E
A L A I   W A R O F W O R D S
B O R N E O   O D O R L E S S
  T E R R A   E R I K
H A Y M A K E R   E T A P E S
A L M A S   T E N S E   L A T
S T E N   I N G O T   P A S O
S E A   A N A I L   D O Y E N
O R L E S S   S A N I T A R Y
    A T O R   N E V E R
S P I R A L E D   S E N O R A
L A S T R E S O R T   C U I R
A R N O   N O R T E   E N D O
W E T   T W E E D   D E W
```

41

```
C L A M P ■ D A N G ■ T O P S
R E G A L ■ E V E R ■ E R I K
O M A N I ■ C O R O L L A R Y
F U N ■ S O L I ■ W A L L I S
T R A N S P A R E N C E ■
■ T E A M ■ Q U E R C U S
S H A H ■ L A Y U P ■ S O S O
O I L ■ ■ T E A ■ R E C
R E A R ■ D O A L L ■ D E S K
B R I E F E R ■ R A T E ■
■ P L A Y W I T H F I R E
T H E A I R ■ A G E R ■ N I X
H E N S T E E T H ■ I L O V E
A S I T ■ S U E T ■ P I N E R
W A D S ■ T A R S ■ S P E N T
```

42

```
T A R E ■ R E E D ■ D A L I
O M A R ■ A I R E R ■ O L I O
G O S S I P C O L U M N I S T
A S P E R S E S ■ A N I T A
■ O E R ■ F A R E ■
S P U R N S ■ M I N K ■ P I P
L E N A ■ P E L E E ■ E R A
E D I T O R I A L W R I T E R
E A T ■ R U N T Y ■ N I N E
P L Y ■ I N K Y ■ C A N T E D
■ F E E S ■ L A M ■
T U R I N ■ M A N I S T E E
S P O R T S R E P O R T E R S
A T O M ■ A U D E N ■ A T I P
R O M A ■ P E E L ■ D E N Y
```

43

```
M A R C ■ V I S A ■ S A S S Y
A M O R ■ I R E S ■ M O C H A
C A P E L L I N I ■ E R R O R
E N E M I E S ■ S A T U R N
■ E N S ■ S A T R A P ■
I A M ■ I T S A B O Y ■ U S A
S P U R N ■ P R O M ■ A L A R
L A S A G N A ■ R A V I O L I
E C C E ■ A R A T ■ A M U S E
T E A ■ P R E S S O N ■ S A L
■ D A R E R S ■ S I S ■
S L I D E S ■ F A S C I S T
H O N E S ■ S P A G H E T T I
I N E P T ■ M I R E ■ N E L L
P E S T O ■ A G E S ■ T R O T
```

44

```
D I S H ■ C H E F ■ D R A M A
I N T O ■ R A R E ■ A U G U R
A G A R ■ E L L A ■ R E A L M
L O R D P E T E R W I M S E Y
■ T E E U P ■ S I N O ■
■ R Y E S ■ E G R E S S
C R I M E ■ C H A N ■ G R I P
R E V U E ■ R E B ■ B U N C O
A D A R ■ G U L L ■ R E S E T
W O N D E R ■ L Y R A ■
■ E V A S ■ A S S E S
A L F R E D H I T C H C O C K
P E R O N ■ I R A K ■ A L E E
S A I N T ■ L A K E ■ L I N G
E S T E S ■ L E E T ■ A C T S
```

45

```
CHAD  METUP  FLEW
HARI  OMANI  LOLA
INEZ  TOPAZ  ICKY
 GAZETTE  ZANIES
   IDLE  BERG
CHANGE  AURA  MOD
HALEY  STRIPMINE
IRIS  POSTA  ERAL
PRESSURES  OZZIE
SYN  EZRA  WIZARD
   HAZY  TINA
SQUALL  TOPKNOT
PULL  ILOVE  IDYL
EINE  NADER  NOPE
CZAR  GROSS  EROS
```

46

```
BRAD  FROG  DWARF
LAME  LEAR  EATER
OBOL  ESTE  CRONE
CALLONTHECARPET
 TEAMS   DADE
     AERO  RENTAL
ELATH  ACHE  TOME
DOAHATCHETJOBON
DIRE  HERR  INERT
AREOLE  EARN
   LOFT  AGANA
READSTHERIOTACT
ARISE  OVID  LORO
MANOR  ROME  AMIR
STUDS  NEAR  SIDE
```

47

```
 ALS  ROAD  COSA
SLUE  SUPRA  AVON
ISAR  WITCHCRAFT
SOUPCONS   ATLAS
  ERRS  GAPE
OPENED  LATERALS
BASTE  RAZOR  BAT
ESTS  HAREM  WORE
ATE  VOIDS  MERGE
HESSIANS  SORTER
  EARS  SHOE
AURAL  STARWARS
BRAMSTOKER  OLEO
BARE  ANILE  LEAD
ALAN  MEDE  FED
```

48

```
 AJAR  OTIS  NOME
INURE  URGE  IRAE
SALIVATION  CALL
ANI  EUDORAWELTY
 AIRTO   TIN
NUCLEO  LIONESS
ASHES  SABRE  ITA
PAIX  PARIS  SMOG
AFL  ZONED  PHONE
 ADMIRES  PEONES
  ONT  ORATE
JOHNCHEEVER  BSA
EVER  OWLISHNESS
TARO  LEAN  ACCRA
SLOE  ERNE  WOKS
```

49

R	A	I	D	■	A	T	T	I	C	■	C	H	A	T
A	S	T	I	■	D	H	O	T	I	■	R	A	K	I
T	H	I	S	H	O	R	R	O	R	M	O	V	I	E
S	Y	N	C	O	P	E	S	■	C	I	N	E	M	A
■	■	R	A	T	E	■	P	U	R	E	■	■	■	■
M	A	C	E	R	S	■	S	A	L	E	S	M	A	N
A	L	A	T	E	■	S	T	R	A	D	■	E	D	E
D	A	N	E	■	S	H	E	E	R	■	M	A	R	S
A	M	O	■	P	H	O	N	E	■	C	A	R	E	I
M	O	N	S	O	O	N	S	■	P	A	J	A	M	A
■	■	H	I	V	E	■	■	W	E	G	O	■	■	■
N	O	S	A	L	E	■	W	H	E	E	L	I	N	G
I	S	T	R	U	L	Y	H	O	R	R	I	B	L	E
K	A	L	E	■	E	M	I	L	E	■	C	A	A	N
E	R	O	S	■	R	A	G	E	D	■	A	R	T	S

50

R	A	S	P	■	A	T	L	A	S	■	S	P	A	T
A	C	H	E	■	B	E	A	D	Y	■	T	I	N	E
P	U	R	R	■	R	A	V	E	N	■	O	N	C	E
■	P	I	C	T	U	R	E	■	■	O	A	K	E	N
■	■	N	E	A	P	■	N	E	X	T	T	O	■	■
A	S	K	N	O	T	■	D	L	I	T	■	F	G	H
S	P	I	T	S	■	P	E	E	P	S	■	C	E	E
T	I	N	S	■	L	A	R	G	E	■	F	O	O	L
E	K	G	■	F	I	S	H	Y	■	F	O	N	D	A
R	E	V	■	A	S	T	I	■	E	L	U	D	E	S
■	■	I	N	S	T	A	L	■	N	E	R	I	■	■
S	C	O	O	T	■	■	L	U	C	A	S	T	A	■
T	U	L	E	■	M	A	M	B	O	■	T	I	N	Y
A	B	E	L	■	S	H	O	E	R	■	A	O	N	E
G	E	T	S	■	S	A	B	R	E	■	R	N	A	S

51

H	A	S	H	■	A	S	S	A	M	■	P	S	S	■
A	L	L	A	H	■	M	A	L	T	A	■	R	I	A
M	O	O	L	A	■	A	M	A	I	N	■	A	M	T
S	P	E	L	L	■	N	O	T	M	Y	T	Y	P	E
■	■	O	F	T	■	V	E	E	■	U	E	L	E	■
W	A	S	A	B	R	O	A	D	■	O	L	D	E	N
A	R	E	■	A	U	E	R	■	R	N	S	■	■	■
S	P	A	N	K	E	R	■	B	E	H	A	V	E	S
■	■	E	E	R	■	E	A	S	E	■	A	T	E	■
S	W	O	R	D	■	I	N	A	T	R	A	N	C	E
A	R	G	O	■	A	N	S	■	S	T	E	■	■	■
F	I	L	L	I	N	G	I	N	■	O	R	O	S	E
E	T	E	■	K	O	A	L	A	■	E	I	N	E	R
T	E	R	■	E	S	T	E	R	■	S	A	T	A	N
Y	R	S	■	S	E	E	D	Y	■	L	O	R	E	■

52

T	O	M	■	F	R	E	T	■	E	R	O	S	E	■
O	P	A	L	■	R	O	M	A	■	L	I	M	I	T
F	E	L	I	C	E	C	A	P	O	D	A	N	N	O
F	R	A	M	E	D	■	N	I	X	■	L	I	E	N
Y	A	R	N	S	■	A	C	R	E	S	■	■	■	■
■	■	■	■	S	E	M	I	■	N	E	A	R	E	D
A	L	O	E	■	R	I	P	S	■	R	H	O	N	E
M	U	M	M	E	R	S	A	N	D	B	A	N	D	S
O	N	A	I	R	■	S	T	A	Y	■	B	A	S	K
S	E	N	L	I	S	■	I	C	E	S	■	■	■	■
■	■	■	K	A	P	O	K	■	E	S	T	E	S	■
I	A	N	S	■	G	I	N	■	L	A	T	E	N	T
S	W	E	A	R	A	N	D	R	E	S	O	L	V	E
I	R	E	N	E	■	T	A	U	S	■	P	L	O	W
T	Y	R	E	S	■	A	Y	R	E	■	S	Y	S	■

53

```
MOWS  ICHOR  DOGS
AREA  MOUTH  OMOO
GILD  MOTHERWELL
MOLDAU  SETASIDE
ANILINE  ROVE
 NEREUS  RESNIK
ANGRY  SOLID  EVA
VATS  COLIC  SEAL
ETO  NOLAN  MARNE
CONCUR  REGARD
 AIRE  RANGOFF
OVERTURN  GNAWER
WELLSPRING  SETA
LALO  TONAL  SLIT
SUES  SLATE  OLDS
```

54

```
BAMBI  STAN  ASHE
OCEAN  PAGE  SHOW
WHENSORROWSCOME
LET  PLY  SCORER
 LEE  REBATERS
THEYCOMENOT
HEART  ARTY  ESSE
RARE  ARIAS  LAIR
URNS  MINI  AORTA
 SINGLESPIES
AMERICAS  RTE
MALAGA  ADO  PAU
BUTINBATTALIONS
IDOL  LIKE  ALONE
TENS  EROS  TALES
```

55

```
ROLL  WAFS  PALE
ONEI  SALON  OKAY
BATTINGPRACTICE
ENTITIES  PRANKS
 GETS  ABIT
SPEARS  CRETONNE
CLAN  SERAI  EEL
AUSTRALIANCRAWL
MME  EMILY  ALEE
PELICANS  PANELS
 CALK  HUMS
ACHING  AIRBOATS
MOUNTAINCLIMBER
APIG  MONKS  EBRO
NETS  SUES  DAMS
```

56

```
JEST  SMOG  BAN
ULNA  LIFE  ALPEN
DIOR  INFO  LUNGE
YAWN  GEE  PARERS
 FISHORCUTBAIT
TILSIT  ORE
AMAHS  SAWS  ERDE
TAKEITORLEAVEIT
ENES  UNES  LACER
 STA  POLITE
PUTUPORSHUTUP
AVATAR  TIN  AINU
RUTTY  POND  TEEN
KLEES  MAGI  ENID
 ARR  STET  STLO
```

57

```
A T P A R   W A G E   C L E W
B R I C E   I M A N   A I R Y
O I L E D   N O S H   S A M E
M E L   C A T S P A J A M A S
B R O C A D E   S N U B
    W I P E R   C L A W E D
M A T T   S I R R E E   E T A
O K A Y S   Z O E   P O T T Y
N I L   A G E N T S   M B A S
A N K A R A   R E G A L
    R A Z E   I N A N A M E
F E A T H E R B E D S   N A M
L A D E   T R A V   B A K I E
U S E R   T E L E   A L E N E
E E N Y   E D E R   G A T E R
```

58

```
G R A B   O P E R A   G L U M
R U B Y   F I N E S   L I R A
I D O L   F U D D Y D U D D Y
D E V I S E   S E R I O U S
    E N T R A P   T E E
A B B E Y   R A W   A R E N T
B O O S   M A Y H E M   V I A
A G A   B A B B I T T   E E N
S E R   O P I A T E   A N C Y
H Y D R O   A C E   A T S E A
    U G H   K N I G H T
F I S S I O N   N E W E S T
O N T H E L E V E L   A V E R
A G E E   E X I L E   R E N E
M E W S   S T I L T   T N T S
```

59

```
B E T A   D O O R S   O H I O
E M I T   A R T I E   C O D A
E I G H T Y F I V E   C U L T
P R E L A T E S   P A U S E S
    E T O   L I B R E
  O F T E N   N I N E S P O T
A R A I   A V E N G E   A L E
M A T C H   E V E   T H R E E
E T H   A S S I S T   A T O M
S E E D L E T S   R O R Y S
    R O L L S   A N D
S E T T E E   B L U E B I R D
O B I T   C E L E B R A T O R
N O M E   T W I N E   C O L E
G E E D   S E P A L   K N E W
```

60

```
I R A S   M I R V   E A S E
B E T H   H A N O I   X R A Y
N A T O   O T T O S   H O S E
  M U R D E R O F C R O W S
      T O R   O A R
C A D E T S   L E N G T H E N
A S A N A   W I L T   E R A
K I N D L E O F K I T T E N S
E D T   V O T E   R E L I T
D E E D L E S S   H U S S E Y
    R O N   A C T
  S L E U T H O F B E A R S
O T I S   F A R O E   B O L T
P A S S   U N D E R   L A I R
T R A Y   L A O S   E M M A
```

225

61

U	R	S	A		E	X	T	R	A		A	L	M	A
R	I	L	E		P	E	R	I	L		N	O	I	R
D	E	A	R		A	B	O	M	I	N	A	B	L	E
U	N	V	A	L	U	E	D		M	O	D	E	L	S
			T	A	L	C		M	E	T	E			
P	O	L	I	C	E		M	I	N	I	M	I	Z	E
I	R	O	N		T	R	E	N	T	O		N	A	G
P	L	U	G	S		O	L	E		N	A	D	I	R
E	O	S		A	N	G	O	R	A		S	U	R	E
S	P	E	C	I	O	U	S		G	A	S	S	E	T
			E	L	S	E		P	I	N	E			
C	A	R	R	O	T		O	I	L	D	R	U	M	S
A	B	H	O	R	R	E	N	C	E		T	R	I	O
T	E	E	N		U	S	U	A	L		E	G	E	R
S	L	O	E		M	E	S	S	Y		D	E	N	T

62

P	R	E	P		P	L	A	I	D		S	P	A	D
R	I	D	E		L	A	I	N	E		L	A	M	E
O	V	E	R	P	A	S	S	E	S		E	S	A	U
F	A	S	T	E	N	S		R	E	P	A	S	T	S
			A	N	E		T	R	A	V	E			
E	N	K	I	N	D	L	E		T	I	E	S	O	N
T	E	E	N	Y		I	N	N	E	R		T	R	Y
A	V	E	S		U	N	D	E	R		F	I	D	E
P	I	P		S	N	E	E	R		A	R	M	E	T
E	L	E	V	E	S		D	O	S	S	I	E	R	S
			R	I	C	E	S		H	O	T			
C	A	P	S	T	A	N		B	A	N	T	E	R	S
H	I	L	O		T	I	M	E	K	E	E	P	E	R
A	D	A	R		E	D	I	L	E		R	E	N	O
D	A	Y	S		D	E	B	A	R		S	E	T	S

63

I	R	S		O	S	M	A	N		P	E	A	C	E
L	E	W		W	H	O	L	E		A	L	L	A	Y
S	E	E		L	O	V	E	F	O	R	L	O	V	E
A	D	E	S		R	I	C		R	E	E	F	E	R
			T	A	S	T	E		S	C	E	N	T	S
W	A	L	R	U	S		S	H	H					
A	V	I	A	N		A	L	A	I	S		C	B	C
D	A	P	H	N	I	S	A	N	D	C	H	L	O	E
E	S	S		A	N	I	T	A		A	H	E	A	D
			T	A	E		S	N	O	O	Z	E		
	S	H	A	R	O	N		A	C	T	U	P		
S	P	I	R	I	T		P	G	A		R	A	C	E
T	A	K	E	T	O	H	E	A	R	T		T	O	M
I	R	E	N	E		A	L	I	C	E		R	O	M
R	E	S	T	S		G	E	N	E	T		A	K	A

64

S	T	A	T		D	O	E	S	T		S	P	A	T
C	A	M	E		E	A	R	T	H		T	R	I	O
I	L	E	D		F	R	E	R	E		A	E	R	O
F	O	N	D	U	E		O	D	E	N	S	E		
I	N	D	E	S	C	R	I	B	A	B	L	E		
			R	E	T	I	R	E		R	E	A	T	A
L	A	S		D	O	D	O		B	O	Y	S	O	F
E	G	A	D		R	E	N	T	A		S	O	D	A
D	E	T	E	R	S		E	R	N	E		N	O	R
A	R	I	C	A		P	R	O	N	T	O			
		R	E	T	R	O	S	P	E	C	T	I	V	E
	L	I	N	E	A	R			R	H	I	N	O	S
F	A	C	T		D	I	O	D	E		O	M	I	T
O	V	A	L		I	N	L	E	T		S	A	L	E
R	E	L	Y		O	G	E	E	S		E	Y	E	R

65

```
A R A M   S C A L A   P A R K
T O M E   P A N E L   O B O E
O W E D   O C T A L   S L A G
M A N I S T H E H U N T E R
    C I T E     D A D
I N T O N E   E L E V A T E D
S A O   G R A C E   E T H E R
L I N G   S O R E R   E U R E
E V I L S   N U K E S   M I A
D E C E I V E S   J A B B E D
    A V E     C O M B
  W O M A N I S H I S G A M E
T A X I   I O W A N   U S E R
A D E N   A N I S E   N E A R
R I N G   L A M E D   S A N S
```

66

```
H A L O   T A M E S   G R A Y
A N I L   A B I D E   U E L E
S T A Y   T R A I L   S P A M
P E R M   A I M E E   S E M E
    P E R S I A N M E L O N
R O S I N S   D I E T
A L I A S   P L A T A   E S P
S P A N I S H O M E L E T T E
H E M   L O O P S   I N N E R
    P E P S   S E D A T E
D A N I S H P A S T R Y
E P I C   I H A T E   M A S T
B A S K   S O R E L   I N C A
T R E E   T R O N A   O S A R
S T I R   S E N O R   N A N A
```

67

```
  O L A V   G A M E   P A T E
A R E C A   A S I N   I L E S
C A N I S   S E N T   C O P S
C L O D H O P P E R   K N E E
    T U E S   E I L E E N
  L A P I N   I R E N E
M A G I   C A S E   E P O D E
E L A P S E D   S T E U B E N
W O R S T   A S T O   S I N G
    Q U A R T   W A S T E
A L B U M S   O V E N
M I L E   S P O I L S P O R T
U V E A   E R G O   W I D E R
S I N K   N O E L   E L I T E
E D D S   T A S S   R E N E
```

68

```
A L E   S P A T   A C T O R
D O L L   A R A R   N O O N E
D I M E S T O R E   S L U M P
U R A N O   V O N S   O R E S
P E N N Y P I N C H E R
    Y A R N   H E M A T I C
B O A   O C S   I N A N E
A T C L O S E Q U A R T E R S
N O R I A   N N E   L E T
K E E P H I S   T O G A
    P U M P E R N I C K E L
S C A M   P A L A   M U N R O
P O L A R   R E C E P T I O N
O P I N E   T M E N   E S S E
T E E N S   A I D S   H E R
```

227

69

```
T O L D   C O T E S   P E E R
A M O R   O S A K A   A T R I
T I N Y   N I V E N   R U I N
I T E R A T E S   D A T I N G
    O V E R   G A L S
B A S T E S   G A L L O P E R
A R C   S C A B   O N I C E
S L O W F A R S L O W G O O D
S E T A E   A P E R   U L A
I N T I M A T E   A R I S E N
    T U N E   S T U N
F L U R R Y   R A I N B O W S
L O S E   O N E T O   O L I O
A G E S   N I N O N   R E E L
P O D S   E D E N S   N O N O
```

70

```
A L O N E   A L S O   C H E W
D E A L T   S I T S   H O L A
M A K E H A S T E S L O W L Y
I C I   S E R A   A R E A S
T H E W A S T E L A N D
    R O N     N E S T E R
S P A I N   L O A N   U R I
W A S T E N O T W A N T N O T
A R T   A N T E   E R A S E
T R I C K Y   S R O
    H A S T Y P U D D I N G
C L O U T   R O L E   N I L
H A S T E M A K E S W A S T E
O G L E   I D E A   S T E R N
W O O D   G E L T   P A T O N
```

71

```
C L E F   A D E L A   H A L L
H E A L   S O W E R   A B I E
I D R A N K W E T C E M E N T
C A N T E E N S   H A M L E T
    C A R Y   L I V E
S A M A R   R I V E T E R S
A D A R E   R A K E   T A I T
L A R   D E A R E S T   T V A
I N I A   L I E N   E M E E R
C O N C R E T E   N E R D S
    T A C T   T H A N
D E S I S T   N O O N T I M E
A N D O H I G O T S T O N E D
R O A N   V A L U E   R I S E
T S K S   E L A P S   S T A N
```

72

```
B A M A   A P R E S   K E T A
E L A M   S H A R P   E G A N
E L L E   C O R G I   R O T O
F I L T R A T E   K A N S A N
    H O P I   F E T E
  P A Y S   C A R N E L I A N
S E N S E D   L O A N   D I E
E R S T   E S T E R   S O M A
A D E   O T T O   D E A L E R
T U R Q U O I S E   A P S E
    U S N R   R A S P
D A K O T A   N O R T H E R S
E M I T   T R A D E   I D E A
L O N E   E A T E N   R I N G
E K E D   S E E S T   E T T E
```

73

```
S I T E ■ C A N E M ■ B L I P
E S O X ■ O L I V A ■ R A N A
A B U T ■ M I D A S T O U C H
M A C R A M E ■ S O A K E R S
■ ■ H E L E N ■ I N R E ■ ■ ■
E T A M I N E ■ V I S I T E D
D I N E T T E ■ E C O N O M Y
N E D ■ ■ ■ ■ ■ ■ ■ U C A
A U G M E N T ■ S P R U C E D
S P O O N E R ■ T R A S H E S
■ ■ D O R E ■ A I M E D ■ ■ ■
I N D I C I A ■ I M P L O D E
T O U C H S T O N E ■ E W E R
U N A U ■ S E D E R ■ S N U G
P A L M ■ A D A R S ■ S S T S
```

74

```
T A C O S ■ M I N A ■ H A R M
I N U R E ■ O R E S ■ O G E E
P O R E D ■ G O E S ■ D A T A
S A L M A G U N D I ■ G R A D
■ ■ ■ T O L A ■ S L E D G E
S L I C E R ■ G E T U P ■ ■ ■
T O T O ■ S E E S ■ L O R I S
E V I N C E D ■ S T U D E N T
M E C C A ■ I D E A ■ G A T E
■ ■ O R D E R ■ S T E P O N
M U S C L E ■ E S T E ■ ■ ■
A B E T ■ M I S C E L L A N Y
R O T I ■ E R S E ■ L A G O S
N A T O ■ A M E N ■ E V A D E
E T O N ■ N A R D ■ R A R E R
```

75

```
E M U S ■ C E S T A ■ L A M B
D A L E ■ U N T I L ■ I L I A
I S L A N D C O N T I N E N T
T H O ■ A D A P T ■ N E E D S
■ ■ F I L M ■ A S A ■ ■ ■
E U C A L Y P T U S T R E E S
A N I L S ■ U S E R ■ A N T
V I T A ■ B A R N S ■ I S N O
E T E ■ C O R K ■ O D E U M
S Y D N E Y A U S T R A L I A
■ ■ O D D ■ H A M S ■ ■ ■
S C U B A ■ G L A R E ■ C H A
A U R O R A A U S T R A L I S
G R A D ■ V I S T A ■ F I J I
A L L Y ■ E T H A N ■ R O O S
```

76

```
■ S T E A M ■ ■ W A S P S ■
S T O R M E R ■ T I P T O E S
H I R S U T E ■ O C T U P L E
A R T ■ R E M A R K S ■ U L E
F R O G ■ S A G O S ■ S L E D
T U N E S ■ I O U ■ D E A R Y
■ P I N K I N G S H E A R S ■
■ ■ U A R ■ ■ I L S ■ ■
■ W H I T E E L E P H A N T ■
S H O N E ■ L O N ■ I L I A D
W I S E ■ R E M A P ■ T O T O
E S T ■ L O V A B L E ■ B T U
E P I T O M E ■ L O R R I E S
P E L I C A N ■ E P I C U R E
■ R E S I N ■ ■ S E A M S ■
```

77

```
SNAPS█SPOUT█ESO
TONIC█LARGO█SOU
ANDTOMORROW█PIE
BEY█FATS███ALLS
███OFTHINGSPAST
PERUSES█OATEN██
EROS███AGRA█ABE
WAITINGFORGODOT
SSS█FOAL███BELA
██TONAL█ARRESTS
THETIMESTHEY███
HERO███ITON█AIM
EXO█PERSISTENCE
FEU█ALTAR█AGNES
TDS█LISLE█LOESS
```

78

```
BOSOM█APSO█ARAL
ALIBI█IRON█POCO
RELIC█DELICIOUS
BOO█REESE█HASTE
███LORDS█GARTER
THROWN█UNIFY███
RIATA█IRANI█MPH
ARM█VETERAN█IOO
YES█ERICA█GETUP
███MOSSO█ADDERS
REMOVE█ORRIS███
ADORE█SKITS█LOS
DETONATED█HOIST
INES█LORE█ERASE
ISLE█LASS█STRAP
```

79

```
SAPS█MALA█SHEAR
ORAL█ATIC█HARRY
PERU█SHEA█IRATE
HARRYHOUDINI███
███POEM█ENS█CCS
ACH█DREAMS█OHIO
THANE█LIU█LIGN
HAROLDMACMILLAN
EPOS█EAT█CADRE
NILE█CRECHE█EST
AND█MOM█AYNS██
██HAROLDPINTER
BRIER█SIGH█OHNE
AUDIT█ELEE█RAID
STORY█TARN█ENDS
```

80

```
CHART█ARLO█SKAT
OATER█NOON█DIDO
ARENA█GOOD█SNIT
LINENDUSTER█GEE
███CAST█CAECUM
LAWMEN█ESKIMO██
ANOA█TORE█SETTO
SNORTER█ALERTED
HALVE█LILY█GOLD
█LENTEN█IRENES
TAYLOR█DUNE███
HUB█RACINGSILKS
ORES█CHAD█IDEAS
SIAM█EINE█GLINT
ECRU█SPAR█NESTS
```

81

```
C I T Y   P L U M E   A C R E
O B I E   R O S I N   M O A N
B E E T H O V E N S T E N T H
A R I   O V I D     I N T R A
L I N E M E N   P O P   R A N
T A S T E   G U R U S   A C C
    H O S   P O I   F R E E
    F I F T H O F J U L Y
T A L C   A I N   A P E
I S E   D R E A M   P E T A L
T I M   I T S   I M I T A T E
A N I S E   E T A S   I R A
N I N E T E E N T H H O L E S
I N G A   P A T E R   H O S E
C E S S   A T O N E   O R T S
```

82

```
S C R A P   I R I S   T E T E
A L U L A   L U N T   A L I T
R O L L S R O Y C E   K L E E
A G E   T I N   A P P E A R S
    T O T A L   P A T
F E D O R A   O V E R H E A D
A R E A S   L A I R   E N D O
C O L S   S O F A S   C A L L
E D I T   O R E L   R A T E L
T E A M S T E R   F A K E R S
    A S H   S C O P E
R O A S T E D   R A T   E L A
E M I T   R A G A M U F F I N
F I D E   N D A K   R O O S T
S T A R   S O M E   E E R I E
```

83

```
S A S H   M U T E S   L A V A
O L E O   I N E R T   A R I D
S A A R   S T A I R   V A S E
O R L A N D O   C A L I B A N
    T O E   A S P E N
C A P I T A L S   S N I P E S
A R L O   L A S S   D A U N T
R I A   A S S E N T S   R T E
T E N O R   T R E E   M E E T
S L O P E S   T E R R I E R S
    H A I L S   M E R
O T H E L L O   P I S A N I O
G O A L   A V E R T   N E A P
L O N I   G E N I E   D O G E
E L S A   E D E N S   A N O N
```

84

```
M I S T   S C O P E   S H E M
A C M E   P O L A R   A U L A
T H E C L O U D S R O L L B Y
H O E   A R L E S   V A L E S
    Q U A E   S A M
C L O U D L E S S C L I M E S
O A S I S   L E A S   I M A
A T A P   J A U N T   T A E L
C H K   F A N S   P H O N E
H E A D I N T H E C L O U D S
    E X E   L I A R
I S T L E   C O U R T   A M E
C L O U D Y A N D C O O L E R
B U R G   A R T E L   W I T S
M E T E   M O O S E   H A Z E
```

85

```
MALORY WAC WALT
ARABIA ASH AGUE
RETOOK STARGELL
CARET THECONSUL
OSA ERR ROWE
  VEREEN ARTIS
ACID AVALON AVA
SHAH DOMES GNAT
KIT FERULA ANNE
STAIR RAKISH
  NEAL NAG AWN
BILLYBUDD NEURO
ALLIANCE HISSER
BEBE EIN ATTEST
USSR RAY DEARTH
```

86

```
LEHAR HAVOC SPA
ELIDE EDITH HUR
NONVIOLENCE AGE
ANTONIO ELLEN
  CELT CORETTA
OGRADY MINSK
MOOT PERDU WEB
NOBELPEACEPRIZE
IDE ISTLE ALIT
  SOARS SHILOH
ATLANTA STAN
DWELL PONDERS
LAO IHAVEADREAM
AIN KARIN LORNE
INA ELECT EPODE
```

87

```
  MINOS RENAN
 DENOTE ELOPED
JONQUIL AVERRED
ANOUNCE DELIVER
BETE NAYS CAME
SETSCREWS VOTED
 SITES AERATED
   AVERTED
 CLASPED FIRED
SHARE REASSURED
PINT MIDI NASA
ANDIRON REPOSED
SEASIDE WAIVERS
 SUTTAS ASSERT
 SEALS YEARS
```

88

```
LADS STEAM SAFE
ANET PANDA ERAT
IDEA EDDAS CIRC
CYMBALS PHARAOH
   LIL STERE
SPEEDILY DETERS
PER ENEMY SERAC
UTAH GIBUS DIVA
MASON SOLES CER
ELEMIS LEMONADE
  OPALS IRE
SURNAME ETERNAL
TREY ACETO VANE
ADAM ROMAN ETNA
BUDS ANELE SOAR
```

89

```
S L A B S █ S C A R █ C O S T
H A V O C █ O A H U █ O L E O
O B E A H █ G L E N █ M I L L
T E R R O R █ M A N I F O L D
█ █ D O O R █ D I D O █ █ █
P A T E L L A S █ N O R M A L
L O A D █ L I A N G █ T A L E
A R C █ I N L A W █ O L D █
I T I S █ N Y A S A █ P R I G
D A T I N G █ D A T E L I N E
█ █ L E S S █ L E N A █ █ █
P R I V A T E S █ R I T U A L
R A V E █ O P A L █ G E S T E
O M A R █ N O V A █ M A S T S
M A N Y █ E Y E D █ A U R A E
```

90

```
S A L T S █ T R I P █ E R A S
A M O R E █ A I N U █ N A S H
L A P I N █ B O C C A C C I O
E T E █ S I L T █ C L O Y E D
M I S S I L E █ L I A R █ █
█ █ I N K █ N O N M E T A L
B R A G G A D O C I O █ A L E
E A R N █ E V A █ K L I N
E K E █ P A P A L N U N C I O
P E A S A N T S █ O N E █ █
█ █ P U T S █ A T T E M P T
U R S U L A █ B R E R █ O L E
C A P R I C C I O █ I O W A N
L I O N █ I O N S █ E R E C T
A N T S █ D O G E █ D A R E S
```

91

```
A N T I █ T H I N G █ T R I P
L O I N █ Y O D E L █ W A C O
A L E F █ C R E T E █ O V E N
N O S E C O N E █ E A T E R Y
█ █ S H O E █ A F R O █ █
B I T T E N █ B L U E N O S E
A M O S █ S P O I L █ E R I C
D A M █ O R E █ G E L █
E G E R █ B L I N D █ S A G A
N O S E G A Y S █ R E N N E T
█ █ G A R P █ G A R O █ █
H O R R O R █ P U G N O S E D
A G E E █ E L L E N █ P O R E
I R I S █ T E A S E █ E T A L
L E N S █ T R Y S T █ D O L L
```

92

```
J E E P █ R E N E █ I M P I
A X L E █ B E G I N █ N O I L
D I S P A R A G E D █ C O N K
E T A █ V U L █ C U B I S T
█ █ D E L I V E R E D █ █
J A P A N E S E █ E D E M A S
A M O I █ E T N A █ S N A R E
M A L L █ S I E N A █ T M E N
B R A Y S █ C E N S █ A B E S
S A R D I S █ R O S E L A K E
█ █ O V E R S T E P S █ █
S Q U A M A █ A R E █ I C E
D A U B █ P L A T T E R F U L
A R I L █ E L V E S █ O N T O
M A Z E █ R Y E S █ W I E N
```

93

```
T A B U . T A T U M . S D A K
I V A N . R I A T A . P I L E
G O L D F I N G E R . I A M A
E N D O R S E . G U N M A N .
. . N E T . A R O L D O . . .
A P P E A R . B E T E L N U T
F I E . K A T E S . E D D Y .
O N A . S M U . E N E . L A P
O T R A . L E T O N . I L E .
T A L L T A L E . T R I L L S
. S P I D E R . T A N . . . .
A L B I N O . H A G G A R D .
N O U N . R U B Y K E E L E R
D I C E . E R O D E . S O D A
I N K S . R I P E N . T E S T
```

94

```
B R U T U S . . C A S S I U S
R E N A T A S . E N T E N T E
E V I D E N T . R E L A T O R
T I P . S T E F A N O . E P A
O L A N . A L O S T . . N I P
N E R O S . A C T . A S S A I
. . D A R T S . H E A R T E N S
. . . T O U R . S I C A . . .
S C H O O L E D . M E T A L .
A H A N D . P O B . D O N O T
R E S . . P U M A S . R A R E
C E T . C O L O N E L . N E A
A T A R L E S . C R E D I T S
S A T I A T E . S I N U A T E
T H E I D E S . . C A E S A R
```

95

```
S H A S T A . . E A T . A M A
H E L P E R . E N C H A S E S
O B L A T E . N E H E M I A H
W E A N . A R G . T R E A T Y
. . I N S O L E . E R N S .
A M U S E . C I N E S I .
P A S H A S . S T A . C H E W
O L E O . A B H O R . A I D A
D O R M . G A M . P A N D E R
. . E R E B U S . S C E N D
. S O L O . A F L C I O . .
A P N E A S . F Y I . F L A B
P A S T R A M I . R E F I N E
T H E S E V E N . C L E A T S
S I T . D E W . E L E M I S
```

96

```
M A P S . A L I B I . S P O T
A L I A . M E S O N . P A C A
C A P T A I N M I D N I G H T
E N S I G N S . L I O N E S S
. . . R E O . T E A R . . . .
A R L E S . S E R . M I S S A
S E E . U R N . F A C I N G
T H E I N V I S I B L E M A N
H A R L O W . I D I . A R E
E B S E N . F O E . S C R E W
. . . E C O N . T E A . . .
O C T A G O N . G A R B L E S
T H E F O R D H A M F L A S H
T A T A . E L I T E . E N T O
O D E R . S E D E R . D E E P
```

97

O	L	G	A		A	M	B	E	R		A	G	R	A
P	O	O	R		N	A	I	V	E		S	E	E	P
A	P	O	L	O	G	I	Z	E	D		T	O	N	E
L	E	N	O	R	E			S	C	A	R	R	E	D
			A	L	A	S		A	G	O	G			
C	O	R	N	C	O	B	P	I	P	E		E	T	C
A	V	A	I	L		U	R	N	S		A	S	I	A
B	U	G	L	E		S	I	T		G	R	A	B	S
A	L	A	E		M	E	N	U		A	N	N	I	E
L	E	M		B	A	S	T	I	L	L	E	D	A	Y
		U	R	A	L		S	T	E	T				
I	N	F	A	N	T	A			V	O	L	L	E	Y
R	A	F	T		H	I	S	P	A	N	I	O	L	A
A	M	I	E		U	N	I	O	N		A	K	I	N
S	E	N	D		S	U	R	A	T		R	I	S	K

98

G	A	S	P		F	O	I	S	T		F	L	A	W
A	M	A	S		I	N	D	I	A		O	A	T	H
F	U	M	E		L	E	A	P	S		O	K	I	E
F	L	O	U	R	I	S	H		S	A	F	E	T	Y
S	E	A	D	O	G		O	P	E	R	A			
		O	A	R	S		A	L	A	R	M	E	D	
S	F	C		N	E	E	D	Y		B	A	I	Z	E
P	O	O	F		E	A	R	O	F		W	E	R	E
E	X	U	R	B		R	U	F	U	S		S	A	D
E	X	P	I	A	T	E		F	R	O	G			
			P	R	A	D	O		B	R	A	Z	O	S
C	A	S	P	A	R		F	R	E	T	W	O	R	K
A	X	L	E		T	O	T	A	L		A	M	B	I
F	E	A	R		A	R	E	S	O		I	B	I	D
E	D	G	Y		R	E	N	E	W		N	A	T	S

99

	P	I	G	S			S	O	L	A	R		
N	A	R	R	O	W		B	A	L	O	N	E	Y
S	E	R	V	I	L	E		O	L	D	T	I	M	E
T	V	A		D	O	S	A	G	E	S		T	A	G
R	A	S	P		S	T	R	U	M		B	R	I	G
A	D	O	R	E		E	M	S		B	R	A	N	S
P	A	L	E	S	T	R	A		C	R	I	S	S	
			S	T	A	N	D	S	O	U	T			
	S	P	E	E	D		I	N	D	I	A	N	A	N
S	P	A	N	S		A	L	E		N	I	O	B	E
C	O	L	T		F	I	L	E	T		N	O	D	E
A	L	A		A	L	D	O	R	A	Y		D	I	D
D	E	V	O	T	E	E		E	N	S	I	L	E	S
S	T	E	E	L	E	D		D	I	E	S	E	L	
	O	R	R	I	S				S	R	A	S		

100

S	P	A	R		S	E	R	G		S	A	U	L
S	O	L	E		P	R	U	N	E		P	U	R	A
S	U	D	A	T	O	R	I	U	M		A	D	I	T
	F	A	S	H	I	O	N		P	A	R	I	S	H
			S	E	L	L		D	O	C	E	T		
F	A	C	E	T			P	A	R	A	S	O	L	S
A	R	A	R	A	T		O	N	I	T		R	I	P
D	E	F	T		H	O	K	K	U		S	I	T	E
E	N	E		P	E	L	E		M	A	T	U	R	E
S	A	T	I	A	T	E	D			N	A	M	E	D
		O	T	A	R	Y		B	R	E	R			
T	A	R	A	R	A		P	R	A	T	T	L	E	
A	N	I	L		M	O	R	A	T	O	R	I	U	M
E	T	U	I		P	R	I	C	E		E	T	R	E
L	A	M	A		B	E	E	R		K	E	E	N

(continued)

John le Carré, *The Secret Pilgrim*
Robert Ludlum, *The Bourne Ultimatum*
Robert Ludlum, *The Road to Omaha*
James A. Michener, *Mexico* (paper)
James A. Michener, *The Novel*
James A. Michener, *The World is My Home* (paper)
Richard North Patterson, *Degree of Guilt*
Louis Phillips, editor, *The Random House Large Print
    Treasury of Best-Loved Poems*
Maria Riva, *Marlene Dietrich* (2 volumes, paper)
Mickey Rooney, *Life Is Too Short*
William Styron, *Darkness Visible*
Margaret Truman, *Murder at the National Cathedral*
Margaret Truman, *Murder at the Pentagon*
Donald Trump with Charles Leerhsen, *Trump: Surviving
    at the Top*
Anne Tyler, *Saint Maybe*
John Updike, *Rabbit at Rest*
Phyllis A. Whitney, *Star Flight* (paper)
Lois Wyse, *Grandchildren Are So Much Fun
    I Should Have Had Them First*

The New York Times Large Print Crossword Puzzles (paper)

Will Weng, editor, Volume 1
Will Weng, editor, Volume 2
Will Weng, editor, Volume 3
Eugene T. Maleska, editor, Volume 4
Eugene T. Maleska, editor, Volume 5
Eugene T. Maleska, editor, Volume 6
Eugene T. Maleska, editor, Volume 7

Eugene T. Maleska, editor, Omnibus Volume 1